The Ascenders

Return To Grace
Book 1

Monty Clayton Ritchings

Copyright

Library and Archives Canada Cataloguing in Publication

Ritchings, Monty 1951 -

The Ascenders Return to Grace Book 1

Monty C. Ritchings

ISBN: 9781738634729

Here's what people are saying about The Ascenders!

"This book is a page turner". Gano

"Intensely interesting modern day fable. I can't wait for the next book!"   DJArtist

"It's about finding your true self and power" " I highly recommend it"   S. Catalano

"A compelling work of remarkable spiritual depth" G. Twa

"The Key To Our Sustainable Future" J. Preuter

Visit us on the web!

www.theascendersbooks.com

www.montyritchings.com

www.youtube.com/powerfulyoupowerfulme

www.powerfulyoupowerfulme.com

Table of Contents

This story has been evolving for thousands of years. Today we start right here!

"Rachel," God whispered. "I have a job for you."

Prologue

"Following the poetry of the sky.
Knowing that Rachel stands nearby,
Rachel waits as she readies the view
She waits to show her love for you."

Mike pondered the recurring dream. He knew Beth was his one. Who the heck is Rachel? Why did she keep showing up in his dreams?

Mike was glad he could share anything with his favorite person, even this odd dream. Beth just smiled confidently, knowingly, as she invited her man to share the story of his younger life.

"It had been a really bad week. My father had been drinking every day like he had so many weeks and months before. I knew this would not end well for us, so I went to my bedroom and got down on my knees. I prayed and prayed. I asked God to please, stop this violence.

It was right around my ninth birthday. I was done. My father was relentless with his fists and anything else he could find to hit Mom and me with."

Mike felt the tears swell as he recalled the pain of those early years.

"The very next day, I was fiddling around out in the backyard when I saw him coming. He was staggering, barely walking. I hoped he would fall to the ground and pass out. He kept coming.

As he neared, I yelled out at him- I control my destiny. You can no longer hurt me.

The next thing I know, my hands are waving in weird ways, pointing at him. He fell like a rock. He lay there with a blissful smile on his face, looking like he had seen God.

I just stood there. I could not believe my eyes. I looked at him. I looked at my hands. They felt like I had stuck one of my fingers in an electrical socket. I didn't care."

Mike looked at his hands as he told Beth the story, recalling that very first time. She leaned over their picnic lunch, giving him a big hug. He smiled and continued, as he clasped her hand. Leaning against a big old cedar tree, he felt the love as the fragrance of his favorite tree wafted up his nose. Even the crystal clear water of the lake he had drawn a million times, seemed to reach out and massage him, carrying away the trauma of the past.

"My father was a changed man. He never hit anyone ever again. In fact, he became quite a likable person. It was awkward at first, but we all made it.

I learned to use this trick well. I did not understand what I was doing, but it did not matter as long as my world was peaceful. The bullies at school became my friends. Other kids started to like me. I could now concentrate on my schoolwork. I found out I was pretty smart."

Then Mike laughed as he pointed at his motorcycle, an all-black vintage Harley-Davidson. "I found my first true love in the traffic department of the City Police. I never did well as a traffic cop, though. People seemed to sense I was sitting there, watching the traffic. The traffic would calm right down every time, so I never got to write many tickets

They sent me to detective school instead. I found the perfect job for this funny little skill.

Speaking of my motorcycle, let's go for a ride!"

Chapter 1

Sitting easily in his favorite place - on the seat of his Harley, he stared at the outside of the local art museum. Mike focused as he drew. He could feel his mind shift, pulling his focus in as the sketch came to life.

"Haven't missed one yet, so let's see what these people tried to pull off."

"Someone has stolen several artifacts from a local museum. They have completely baffled police, as there is no evidence of the crime occurring," was the way the news reporters had put it.

Mike knew there were always clues, often so obvious they get missed. He rested as he drew the building where the crime had taken place. As he drew it, he became bonded with the drawing. Pictures flowed to him. Before long, he had conjured up the information he needed -who had committed the crime and how. The faces of the men involved, the plundered goods, even the vehicle they had escaped in, all found their way onto the paper.

With Mike's evidence in hand, the perps soon found themselves in jail.

"Another day in paradise". He mused as he shifted his Harley into gear--- off for a celebratory ride. He thrust his fist into the air as another victory settled in.

***

A few days later, he was sitting on his motorcycle outside of another crime scene doing his best to conjure up the story. He was distracted by two mean looking men walking toward him. They were carrying baseball bats, intending to put him out of business.

Mike watched the men approaching. With a wave of his arms, he did his secret gesture as he murmured his special words. The men stopped in their tracks, not knowing what had happened to them. Dropping their clubs, as their legs became weak, they fell to the ground. Their days of crime were over.

Mike continued his work, clearing up the backlog of cold cases, one by one.

***

The two TV news reporters had found out the identity of this mystery person who was busy cleaning up these impossible cases. Blaring on televisions all over the city--- a picture portraying Mike sitting on his motorcycle!

Limelight and popularity were not on his bucket list. He did not need attention from the public in this kind of work. Being invisible was an important asset. He needed the quiet to relax and connect. He was relieved they knew nothing about his art or his special ability to diffuse situations.

Solving these crimes with people hanging around made the situation unbearable, making the process far too challenging. Some people waited for days at crime scenes just to get a look at him working. They had become a real nuisance.

He plied his trade but began finding the interference became too much.

As his popularity increased, he started suffering from headaches. Little ones at first, only lasting for seconds, but they were getting worse.

***

As Mike grew up, his skill in using the technique grew as well. He had learned to use it to protect himself in various ways. As he applied it, he became a very confident person who felt safe and thus enjoyed his special life.

Work was not the only use for this unique skill, it had a fun side to it, too. Mike loved to doodle when he had nothing pressing in the moment. It was like going off into space. His skill as an artist merged with his skill of thought projecting. His art came to life!

On one of his favorite walks near his home, the lake would come to life on his paper. With pen in hand, he drew the bullrushes blossoming; the ducks resting together, and the water rippling from the gentle breeze. After he had sketched the full beauty of this nature, he would use his mind to alter the scene to show the same ducks flying.

The creatures, astounded, found themselves airborne without having lifted a wing. He was giddy with laughter as the birds, red-cheeked with embarrassment, regained control and flew off, never understanding what had taken place.

During his career in law enforcement, he had many opportunities to meld his intuitive skills with his special artistry, which helped him to become recognized as a top-rated investigator.

One day, as Mike was walking in the forest, he noticed something odd. A spot on the forest floor appeared to have become a small burial site. Mike's eyes poured over the situation. He noticed how someone had turned the soil and how they had replaced the leaves in such an orderly manner.

His experience had taught him to leave things be, so he just stared at the spot. Soon he saw pictures forming in his mind.

Mike knew the pictures were clues. There was a box of jewelry buried in the ground, waiting to be retrieved. As the pictures of the thief appeared, he recalled this person from his bygone days on the force. He would recognize that scruffy face anywhere.

Mike called his buddies, and soon enough, that face was behind bars, and the jewelry returned to the rightful owner.

***

Word in the law enforcement community spread like wildfire about how Mike had solved this crime without one actual piece of evidence.

Mike soon recognized his career was over. He needed to move on.

It was time for a long vacation. He wanted to take some time to decide what was next for him.

His favorite confidant, Beth, encouraged him to just relax, maybe go for long walks while he reflected on his prospects. He could sense something exciting was in his near future.

***

It did not take long. His phone rang.

It was the vice president of the investigation department of a large insurance company.

The next day, Mike flew to the company's corporate headquarters. They handed him a simple piece of paper. It was to develop into a very lucrative contract that would make him a lot of money for many years to come.

He was still feeling hesitant about being drawn back into the world of bureaucracies, but the clincher was when they presented him with the keys to his dream motorcycle, a restored vintage midnight black Harley-Davidson. Who could say no?

Return flight canceled. His new career had started as the wind blew in his face on the return home.

This suited Mike just fine, as long as he could turn the perps over to the police. It was his belief that God created some people to do paperwork. They called themselves police officers. Mike was a person of action. To him, pens were for drawing.

His life got exciting fast!

Mike continued building his successful career, honing his skills into his unique art form; developing an amazing skill at reading into his art. The pictures just flowed from his mind, like watching a movie.

The bad guys didn't have a chance.

Mike relished every moment. Money was no obstacle now. He worked half as hard, so had plenty of time for his many hobbies. He settled himself into a comfy home in the country... just so he could be close enough to enjoy the one thing that constantly uplifted him... Nature. His bond with any of the plants re-energized him anywhere he walked.

As his life progressed, even this career soon left him behind. His life awaited before him, just on the horizon. There were much bigger opportunities for Mike and his special skills. However, these headaches needed to be dealt with before anything else. The pounding in his head was getting worse.

Chapter 2

In the dream, he was dancing freely, swirling around the room, wearing a loose-fitting sheer dress that floated in the air with the flow of the music. He was so free. Burning inside was a power that he had never known in the awake world, waiting.

The same dream occurred night after night until one day Mike realized it was a message.

The headaches got worse. Never enough to be debilitating, but definitely becoming irritating. Finally, he confessed to Beth.

"I thought you were just reminiscing."

They truly loved each other. Their relationship had blossomed over the time they had been together, but they enjoyed having separate residences, although she was well prepared for long stays at his home. Lucky for him.

Well into her practice, she met him. The police had called her to help deal with a family of kids whose parents had been murdered right in front of them.

Beth immediately recalled her own traumatic childhood as she comforted the helpless children, struggling to maintain her composure. As Mike continued his own investigation, he understood her sadness, so he came over to give this beautiful person some emotional support. They never looked back.

Slipping into his bedroom, she called, "Come in here please, sweetie."

Mike entered his bedroom, wondering what his favorite lady was doing. He saw a pair of black lace panties and a matching full slip laying on the bed.

"Put these on," she whispered as she turned back to the closet.

"I know who you are deep inside. What you wear for clothes does not change you. I love you and want you to do what you have to. Those headaches have to go. If wearing female clothing stops them, then that will have to do for now."

She smiled as she saw him pulling the long, full slip down over the beautiful panties. To reassure him, she moved up to him, hugged him tightly, and handed him a silky, black, knee-length dress.

As she moved away from the closet, he became visible in the mirror. Mike realized he had found some relief.

He stood there looking at himself for a moment. He took slow, calming breaths, still unsure what to make of the situation. As he calmed down, his energy was different. It was a whole new level of power. He recalled the dream.

"I cannot make sense of this. Since I learned how to work with this energy, I have always been comfortable with myself, confident, and in my body. Now I get something that is more powerful and pleasant than I have ever known before. I like it, but I still don't get why it requires me to dress in your clothes."

***

Though Beth supported him by buying him nice clothing, he could not manage the headaches when away from home.

His male ego was too strong. He would not wear dresses outside the house, not even panties, although he had embraced the pleasure of wearing what she provided for him while at home. He feared others might consider him a freak. Even world-famous detectives need to fit in sometimes.

***

Finally, the headaches were too much. They were pounding so hard inside his head. He was getting to a point where he could not drive his motorcycle safely to work on his cases. Something had to be done.

He visited his doctor, who referred him to an endocrinologist. It was no help. All the tests showed his body was operating normally, although there was certainly wear and tear showing from the headaches he was suffering.

Doctor after doctor could offer no help. It completely baffled them. Any medications were either rejected by his body or just did nothing. Talk about frustrating.

Finally, Beth suggested Mike make an appointment with Sheila. He thought this kind of strange that he should visit a child trauma counselor, but he finally agreed. His suffering needed to stop.

Sheila worked with him in the same way she counseled any young person. Through her, he resolved many of his childhood issues. He was grateful, but the headaches continued.

Throughout the sessions, he recounted the terror that his father had subjected him and his mother to during his early years and learned to be at peace.

Sheila provided the medium for Mike to let his fear have a voice. It was a lot of work requiring a great deal of patience for him to find the innocent child that hid in the shadows of all the violence that had become his history.

She wondered how he had endured at all. One day, he spoke about the amazing gift that came to him through the power of prayer. She learned he had always had a leaning toward the mystical life. It was not surprising that his psychic gifts had expressed.

These unique powers were a lifesaver. However, this work was not enough to stop the headaches.

One day, while Mike worked on some exercises she had given him, Sheila chatted with Beth; Mike's lady, her friend, and now co-worker. She had come a long way in her own healing journey. Now she hoped the same for this incredible man.

***

"I was raised for the first nine years in a faraway city that wars had ravaged for a long time. My parents were wealthy business people who were suspected of being complicit with a group trying to oust the country's current political regime. They dearly loved me, but now was the time to oust the riff-raff currently in office. There was nothing too great to sacrifice for the cause.

One day, this life ended as an explosion destroyed the building that housed my parents' office. They were both killed.

Fortunately for me, this group was ready for every eventuality. I was in the care of these people so that before the fire was even out, I was spirited out of the country. My new life began in a loving home far, far away from anyone I had ever known.

I knew and understood what had happened, but was so traumatized that I never spoke a word for many months. Although I could speak both my native tongue and English well, I spoke not a word. There was no point in me going to school, so I just sat in my room by myself all day for so many months. Just a girl lost in a jungle of emotions.

Finally, my new parents introduced me to you. My world changed that day."

"Yes, I recall that day vividly, my friend. It took a long time, but eventually, your eyes shone again. As the protective barriers melted, you relaxed. Then was the day you started crying. The door to your prison finally opened, and the healing began."

"Yes, it was only a few more months, and I was ready to rejoin the world. My parents enrolled me at a private school near home, and my new life began."

"I was so glad you continued your relationship with me, You were such a fine mentor for the other children. And now here you are, a full-fledged counselor working right at my side. I am betting we have a lot more amazing work to do together yet, my friend." Sheila pulled Beth into her for a big long hug.

***

Noticing that Mike had finished the exercise, Sheila read it through searching for answers. On completion, she looked at Mike and said. " This exercise was designed to help me determine where you are at at this stage. Whatever it is that is causing these terrible headaches has nothing to do with the events of your childhood. While you were working, Beth and I discussed the situation and have come to the conclusion that we need to pass you along to a person who can take a different approach. We are quite sure she can help you."

***

As Mike entered the treatment room, he tried to relax. This was pretty easy, as the calming influence of the scent of lavender flowed into his nostrils. It was the first time in a very long, grueling time that it seemed like he was going to get better.

When the medium entered the room, she immediately froze in her steps as she looked at Mike. Reality was finally here as this man sat before her. She stuttered as she said she needed a moment more and retreated into her office.

She sat down in shock. She did deep breaths to calm herself and to get grounded.

Finally, after about five minutes, she stood up and slowly re-entered the room, where Mike patiently sat.

The next stage of his life was about to begin!

***

As they connected, they made small talk about life. Mike mentioned that he really liked the scent of the lavender she misted into the air.

The perfect opening... Rose launched in.

"I have not misted the air with lavender... or any other scent. I do not allow artificial information to be used in the room as it could interfere with accessing important information."

Mike stared at her in wonder and disbelief. He knew he could smell lavender. He wondered if he should believe her. So many crazy and unexplainable events had happened to him in recent times though, so he just accepted what she said, shrugged his shoulders, and relaxed. This was just one more!

Rose explained, "The lavender is present for you because it is how one of your spirit guides announces themselves. This entity that is attempting to communicate with you is very strong and important.

One can tell this by the fragrance they express. Lavender is number one.

She asked Mike if he was ready to meet this guide. Mike agreed, trusting what she told him.

Rose led Mike into a communion trance. He did not exactly understand what was happening, but as he relaxed and accepted; he and Rose immediately saw her in their minds.

She was big and beautiful with long, curly blond hair. She wore a majestic lavender floor-length gown.

"*I am Rachel. I am your Guardian Angel, Michael,*" she whispered.

Rachel looked at Mike, then at Rose, then back at Mike. She smiled the warmest, most radiant smile he had ever enjoyed. Mike understood the dream.

"*I have long been with you, Michael, as you walked through the trials of your life. It is now time for us to work together in consciousness. If you should agree, Rose will be your mentor and Guide. She will provide you with some very important information about how your life is going to be from now on. Do you accept Michael?*"

Mike nodded immediately and returned his own glowing smile. The cause of his headaches was about to be revealed.

"Both Rose and I will work with you for the rest of your life. Your parents aptly named you after Archangel Michael, my dear one. Like your namesake, we are going to do some amazing work that will change the world."

***

Over time, Rachel would guide the group through Rose. She needed to ensure that the day-to-day changes were being implemented as required. She said she would also periodically appear when needed to provide guidance.

Curious, but still with a headache, Mike sat and listened. A calmness overcame him. He trusted what was happening. They all sat quietly for several moments in contemplation of what was occurring.

Finally, Rose spoke. "Mike, please speak about your thoughts and feelings about what has now happened. Are you ready to begin?"

All Mike could do was smile. It was as if he had taken a drug taking him to a place where he had never been before. Rose began explaining, even though Mike was still in bliss.

"You and I are members of a new kind of human species. Most people are Homo Sapiens. There are also others like us, who we will help to discover their true identity.

This new species is Homo integratis.

Whether they accept it, all humans have both male and female aspects of their being. We all express both male and female traits; however, usually whichever gender our body is, would be the dominant expression."

Mike sat, completely entranced by the information Rose revealed. Things were now making sense.

"Our souls do not have genders. A soul is universal and beyond the characteristics of our existing plane of consciousness. Over our many lifetimes, we express in either a male or a female body, depending on what we need to learn in that lifetime.

Whatever gender we are born into has specific learning opportunities, much the same as ethnicity, family situation, geographical location, health condition, intelligence, and other characteristics created to provide the arena for that period's learning opportunities.

We, who are Homo integratis, have the unique ability to shift our physical bodies from male to female as the situation arises. This allows and supports us to do powerful work using either gender's unique strengths more fully.

When the task at hand is done, we always return to the gender of the body of this incarnation and remain so when not working on a specific project that better suits the other gender. The job at hand now is for you to learn how to let your female expression appear, then to let her breathe a new breath into your being.

This process will take a while, but if you let it, you will live a life beyond anyone's belief."

Mike sat, almost comatose... then with no resistance, he accepted his new life. Instantly, the headaches disappeared.

Slowly, Rose lifted a large mirror she had placed on the table before Mike had arrived. As the mirror became vertical, Mike stared into it, amazed! Rather than seeing his own face, he saw a female who looked like she could be his sister.

Mike stared into the mirror, shocked. There were no words or feelings to express how this situation felt, but being Mike, he just went with it as long as those headaches were gone

Just for fun, he began making faces at his reflection. She responded in like. It truly was him, or should we say... her? His other half was looking back at him.

She let him know the headaches had been her way of telling him she existed... and wanted out! They laughed and laughed as everyone accepted their new life and reality.

Chapter 3

Although Merle (Mare-la) had appeared so she could introduce herself, there was much training for her to do to express herself in the outer world, and do the work she needed to do.

This kind of sharing was new to Mike. This was sharing at the highest level, to a point that no other person has ever needed to be so generous before. Can you imagine?

"The first lesson for you, Mike, is to learn how to move your Kundalini energy," Rachel spoke through Rose. *"I will assist you at first. You will need to learn how to do it yourself. This technique will help you manage and work with the amazing amount of energy that is going to be flowing through your being."*

Mike looked puzzled. He knew about working with universal energy. He had not come across the term Kundalini.

"Kundalini energy refers to the female energy that lies latent in the tailbone until a person accepts their spiritual nature and knows they connect with Source. Acceptance supports the Kundalini energy to

move up the spine to reconnect and expand throughout the individual's entire being.

With the increasing demand from Source for recognition, along with the need for the implementation of this energy, many people are developing health issues because the energy is becoming strong and demanding, while these individuals continue to ignore and suppress it. This energy will not be ignored, as many spinal issues plus diseases like diabetes can be attributed.

Meditation and visualization practice will help you learn to move the energy up your spine and connect with Source in this manner.

Practice will help you become proficient in moving the energy. This will support Merle to become stronger, allowing her to transition your being so that she can appear with no struggle when needed."

"Beyond relieving these headaches, why do I need to be two people? The changes I have embraced have made my life confusing enough without having Merle in my life."

"The greatest mistake humans have ever perpetrated on their species is degenderizing themselves. *The Universe created men and women differently on purpose. Nothing is ever by accident, or without necessity.*

This obsession to diffuse the differences between the genders has come to light only in recent years. It has been a costly mistake. It seems neither sex knows who they are anymore. The result being a dramatic increase in gender-based diseases and a general loss in clarity of self-awareness.

Women have assumed their power by taking a male perspective rather than becoming powerful using their female mind, while men have become fearful of doing anything for fear of being reprimanded, therefore costing them the expression of their masculine nature.

Our first step in helping you to work in both genders as separate individuals requires you to have clarity in the difference between the two. Each gender on its own is powerful in its own beautiful way, so your job is to just relax and become.

You already work well with Merle. She is the one who gives you the information you need to solve the crimes. It is appropriate that they blessed her with her name, as she has already shown that, as her name implies, she is intelligent, strong, and quick-witted. It will do you well to give great respect to her."

"So why do I need to be around then, if she is doing all the work?"

"She doesn't know how to drive motorcycles!" laughed Rachel teasingly.

"No, please understand, male energy is more grounded and therefore carries the energy better than a female body for working on the earth plane. Female energy is stronger when working with Source while performing such activities as channeling or expressing personal power through the mind.

Even when Merle is expressing, she is doing it through your body. You hold the ground for her, so the work is completed on earth plane. Without you, her work would stay on a more ethereal level. Since we are working with very new intense energy, you are her grounding rod, so to speak.

You cannot reach the levels of attunement with Source like Merle because female energy is more passive, therefore more able to receive than the action-based male energy. You have become the perfect combination... or at least will be soon when you finish integrating."

"So, what is the next step? I am not sure if I completely understand, but I trust that this is where I need to go. Oh, one more question.

If so many people are having issues in their bodies because of the stagnant Kundalini energy, will they become like me, when they release it?"

"Good question Michael! The simple answer is no. Most of the current population are Homo Sapiens, and in that, they are incapable of rising to this level of expression at this time. When one learns to tap into the Kundalini energy and helping it to express will help them improve their health. They may also start to search for answers about their purpose in life, and desire to commune with Source.

There are many more Homo integratis who will discover their uniqueness along the way. For now, the majority will just become more spiritual. It takes a very evolved soul to handle what we are doing. You should feel honored, Michael.

Let us begin the lessons now. You need to become adept with this process as quick as you can.

*After all, we don't want Merle to become impatient
again, do we?*

*The first lesson relates to your diet. You are a
healthy eater. For now, it is acceptable for you to eat
such things as meats and desserts. As your energy
rises you will find that it will impede the flow of the
energy. You need meat now because you need to
keep yourself grounded. As your system adapts to
this new life, you may discover that all your food
tastes sweet, so your desire for sugar will dissipate
and even a vegetarian diet will be sufficient.*

*It is good to love what you choose to eat.
Remember that before you eat, take time to relax and
connect with your food. It is the reason the ancient
priests created the concept of Grace. Take the time to
be grateful for what you receive and allow yourself to
connect with the food, so eating your food becomes a
pleasure, and you gain the most value from it."*

"How do I connect with the food?"

*"You sit in the quiet for a moment or two while
sitting in front of the food, with no distractions. When
you feel calm, place your hands above the food in
front of you, palms down, and visualize projecting*

energy from your hands which connects with the energy of the food.

You close your eyes and say a brief prayer of thanks to the food and the plants or animals that have given their lives for you to prosper, then put your hands down beside the dish. After a moment, enjoy your meal.

Your next step is breathing. Most humans do not breathe as they were intended. Their lungs never release the toxins they breathe in, so how can they expect their bodies to be free of these poisons?

Your abdominal muscles must move with each breath.

There are three levels to your lungs. The bottom of the lungs is where the toxins lie. If they remain, when the blood passes through to re-oxygenate, the blood refuels with toxins instead of oxygen. Take a deep breath, making sure your belly moves for me right now please, Michael."

Mike did as requested, taking slow breaths, making sure his belly rose with the breath. He took as deep a breath as he could, then held it and then released it in the same manner. Mike took the time to relax when he finished. He waited for Rachel to speak again.

"That was perfect Michael. Now breathe at a normal rate, doing the same. Every time you breathe, the abdominal muscles need to be engaged, no matter how deep the breath.

You will find you have more energy, and you think better once this style of breathing becomes a habit. Correct breathing is also easier by sitting in a position with a straight back and shoulders to allow more room for the lungs to perform as designed, making it easier to breathe. Comfort is essential though."

"Those are pretty simple changes to accommodate. Thank you, Rachel."

"And that leads us to lesson three, appreciation and gratitude.

Human bodies are amazing machines with complex inner systems. The most significant of the systems for our purpose is the Endocrine System. Its purpose is to regulate the metabolic state of the body. It is always trying to maintain what we call homeostasis or in layman's terms- Balance.

Appreciation and gratitude are key attributes needed for maintaining homeostasis. They cause the energy of the body to open and to expand, allowing Universal energy to absorb and release with minimal effort. This allows the glands and organs that comprise the Endocrine System to do their jobs as well.

When appreciation and gratitude are excluded, the body becomes heavier; the mind becomes cloudy and as the congested energy accumulates, illness prevails. Trust me, a little appreciation goes a long way.

The exercise for you now, Michael, is to become appreciation and gratitude embodied. Reach out to help others with no expectation of reward. Speak your appreciation of all that happens in your daily journey, even the stuff you don't like. You will soon realize, there is a gift in every single thing.

That is a lot for you to digest for now, Michael. We need to be careful we do not tire ourselves in this process. Please take some time to rest and go for a walk in the forest. We will continue later."

With the lesson finished, Rachel faded back into the ethers.

Mike sat for a long while. He pondered about how his life had become so special because of this gift, and now he understood and gave thanks to the one who had been the channel for his wonderful power and saved his life so many years before.

He let his mind wander. He had become a police officer after completing college. The training was challenging, but he felt it was his calling. In only a few years, he had worked in almost every division of the local police force, trying to find his place.

In the traffic department, he had found his first true love... motorcycles.

He had transferred out of traffic, though, because he never made the required quota of tickets. As he was sitting on his motorcycle watching for misbehaving drivers, he realized wherever he sat, the traffic slowed down and behaved itself. This power that had been gifted to him working in strange ways. His need to write traffic tickets went unfulfilled.

After many years and by working his way through the many departments, Mike became a detective. This was a job made for him! Like a bolt of lightning, he became the top-rated detective in his office, and soon on the entire force. Crimes were easy to solve for Mike.

He would just draw the crime scene and the information would flow. The evidence revealed itself once he knew what had happened. It was little effort for this guy to put the bad guys behind bars.

His supervisors were dumbfounded. They had seen no one like him before.

Much to their dismay, Mike soon realized he had put up with enough of policing and bureaucracies, so he quit. He knew it was the right decision.

This life needed to breathe. So did Merle. He sat smiling in his tranquility, ever thankful.

Chapter 4

As Mike wandered slowly in the forest, he stopped often to visit with his plant friends, embracing their energy by admiring their leaves and flowers, stroking them gently. If there was one thing that had saved him as a child, it was his love for plants! He did not send them birthday cards... but close!

"Boy, and people thought I was weird before! Wait till they check out the new me! If you think having plants for friends is weird, let me tell you guys!" Mike laughed as he sauntered along.

Mike had realized quite some time ago that another facet of his special skills was that he could connect with plant energy. Today he had been through a lot. It had been emotionally difficult. As he walked, he focused his mind to attract a plant that contained healing energy for the nervous system... And as fast as he focused on it, there before him was his friend, the St. John's Wort.

Mike touched the plant fondly and communed with its energy until the nervine that flowed through its cells fed his poor nerves. Slowly, he breathed it in until he was completely relaxed. As usual, in appreciation to his friend, he tousled the plant's head, said thanks, and carried on with his walk.

Whistling happily as he walked along, he almost ran right smack into his love. She had seen him and let herself slide into his arms as he walked into her arms, giving him a great big hug and kiss. Mike closed his arms around her as he snuggled into the hug.

When they separated, he studied her face, spewing, "What a pleasant surprise. What are you doing in my neck of the woods?"

She grinned at him, saying nothing for a moment. Then, she announced, "I am accompanying you in your afternoon session."

He stared. He waited until she went on, as he was confident she would.

"I have a confession. I apologize in advance that I have not explained this to you before, but they directed me to play dumb."

He could not seem to make sense of this new revelation.

"What are you saying? Why are you accompanying me in my class?" This man could hardly believe this admission.

"I too am a Homo integratis, only female based. Sheila suspected it quite a while ago, but it was not the appropriate occasion to talk about it. Recently, she advised me to meet with Rose.

She already briefed her about me, so there was no shock when I stepped through the door. She informed me about your headaches, the temporary solution... and the actual solution. I am sorry you had to suffer so much to get to this point, but, my love, we are here now. She said it stunned her when she saw you on that initial session, because she could see Merle peering out psychically already.

I have been waiting so long for this moment to arrive, so we can walk this journey together. I need to understand how to release the Kundalini too! Now, if you are okay with it, we should get back to Rose. I am sure Rachel will be waiting."

Mike looked at Beth again, yet in shock, but he had a very affectionate and amused look on his face.

"I love you, Beth. You never cease to astound me. I am so relieved that we are continuing on this journey together," he replied, as a tear rolled down his cheek.

***

They arrived back at Rose's office to find her already sitting in her seat, grinning like a Cheshire cat. She was so pleased with herself and with Beth for pulling this off, she almost jumped out of her skin. Instead, she rushed to the pair, giving them one big lavender scented hug, pulling them both in really tight to her.

When they were seated, she began the new session, still snickering.

"Now that we are all here, we will learn how to bring up our Kundalini through our spine. Rachel has suggested that I should perform this lesson today.

Our first step in doing any esoteric practice is to pay credence to the Cosmic. Gently wash your hands, and have a drink of water. This is a sign of supplication or recognition of Source.

The next step is settling into a comfortable position. Whether you park yourself in a chair with your feet flat on the ground or if you choose to sit in lotus position, make sure you are comfortable and that your spine is relatively straight.

Following this aspect is the breathing. Remember to breathe by moving your belly so that your breaths are deep and complete. We do what we call positive breathing for this.

We accomplish this by taking in a full, deep breath, holding it for a short time, then slowly releasing it. We repeat this throughout.

As you breathe in, chant, 'hoong' silently on the in breath. Hold. As you slowly breathe out, you chant 'Sau' (saw) for the entire exhale.

As you repeat this process, allow your senses to connect with the Kundalini unraveling in your tailbone, so that as you proceed, it rises up your spine.

In traditional Hindu practice, they release the energy through the third eye in the center of your forehead. For our purpose, allow it to travel upward and rise out of the Crown Chakra at the center of the top of your head. This allows this energy to reconnect with the Cosmic via the Star Chakra, which is 18 inches above your head, in your auric field.

Make each round as long as you can, but try for at least 15-20 minutes. As you progress and learn the value of this exercise, you will continue the meditation for longer periods, even hours, not realizing it.

Your most important task right now, Michael, is that you master this tool right away so that Merle can become more active on the outside. Go ahead and begin. See you later."

Mike made for his trusty pen and paper, but Rose snapped it away before he could get it, causing it to fly off the table.

Astonished, he looked at her, being a bit whiney. "Why can't I just draw the Kundalini energy traveling up our spines? We can all be good to go in about 10 minutes."

Calmly, she grinned. "This talent of yours is a blessing and a curse. You wave your hands, and voila, it is yours.

You are going to start working through things the way we others have to... with a tool called practice. Do you recall being advised that one of your male attributes that is essential to this relationship is being grounded?"

Mike sounded like a schoolboy being scolded. "Yes Rose, I do."

"Well, this is the beginning of the grounding process. You will have to accept doing things the old-fashioned way.

Rose went on. "For you to be truly grounded, so you can carry this kind of energy, you need to be one with your body. It is an interesting fact that is true for all people... for one to be truly in their own power, they must first be comfortable in their own body. We will go into this in detail later."

Rose prepared herself for meditation by moving into the lotus position. She focused on her breathing. Taking the cue, they followed her.

Mike found himself tempted to move the energy anyway, but he had agreed to follow Rose's teachings. He closed his eyes to focus on his breathing. As he surrendered, his last memory of the outside world was the soft, deliberate breaths of the others, as they moved into their zone.

Chapter 5

"Where am I? I thought I was doing a visualization, but I am here, wherever here is."

Mike scanned the room. He was in a snuggly cocoon, a safe place to explore. He had traveled out of his body many times before, but this was a whole new experience.

As he chatted with himself, he realized the presence of another being. As she approached him, his body energy soared to an unprecedented height. It was Merle.

She appeared before him dressed in the beautiful black outfit that Beth had put together for him that first evening when they were trying to manage his headaches. She beamed at him as she sat down, facing him.

She moved into meditation position, closed her eyes, and began breathing in concert with Mike's breath. Inside his mind, Mike closed his eyes again and joined her.

They bonded energetically. Merle set the pace for their breathing. Measured breaths in, full positive breaths, chanting "Hoong". Holding breaths for as long as comfortable. Slow breaths out, chanting "Sau."

Mike struggled to keep focus. His mind rebelled. It went from motorcycle rides to recalling cold cases, to making love with Beth. He kept breathing, struggling to refocus.

Merle reached over and placed her hands on his, letting his mind calm down so focus became easy. As he concentrated, the energy stirred, hot and angry, as it nestled in his tailbone. Hot lava in a volcano, waiting to explode into the air.

He craved to release it, allow it to flow up his spine, and watch it spew into the air above his head, but it remained still. He relaxed and began refocusing on his breathing again, but his mind preferred to escape. It took him back to riding motorcycles and solving cold cases and making love with Beth, anywhere except to the job at hand.

Merle continued to hold his hand; he calmed himself and refocused again on his breath. The energy gushed up his spine as Merle's hand relaxed on his. He let go.

Sometime later, Mike opened his eyes. As he regained his sight, he knew both ladies were staring at him, smiling.

"Well, aren't you the showoff, Michael!" Rose chided. "We have been sitting here chatting for, oh, about forty-five minutes, since we returned. We thought you might like it there so much that you chose to remain inside permanently."

"By the way, it was lovely watching your Kundalini energy spurting out the top of your head. Pretty good for the first time!"

Mike looked sheepishly at both ladies. "I had help. My mind was not going anywhere near this business, but Merle came and sat with me. As soon as she put her hands on mine, I was a goner!"

"Now you have officially experienced true Kundalini energy, and you have it loosened up enough, so next time, Merle can relax and let you do it on your own!" Beth laughed with mischievous joy at Mike.

***

It had been a wonderful day, so Mike and Beth decided they would celebrate their victories.

"Let's dine at our favorite little Italian Bistro tonight. You know the one over by your place, Sweetie."

Mike smiled as he caught the nuance... No sleeping alone tonight.

As they relaxed at the Bistro, they enjoyed some red wine and coconut shrimp as they chatted. It was certainly a day to remember... one of many to come.

"It would be fabulous to jump into bed when we get back home tonight, but I am wondering if you are getting the same sense as me...." Mike whispered.

"You mean we should savor today's work, and not convert it into sexual energy? We are both on the same page, my dear. We will have other opportunities to enjoy our luscious bonding."

When they arrived back at his place, it was getting late, but they were too excited to bring this day to a close. Instead of their usual Scrabble tournament, with Mike being thoroughly trounced, he dug out his Karaoke CDs.

"This could be a pleasant way for us to bond. Let's sing some duets," he said, as he poured through his collection, looking for the perfect CD.

"You are such a romantic," Beth giggled as she started warming her voice up.

Two hours and a million songs later, it was finally time for bed. They peered at each other through sleepy eyes, spontaneously singing the same lullaby.

"God, we certainly do know each other well, don't we," she quipped, sliding into the bed beside her man.

As fast as the light faded out, both were deep asleep. At some point during the night, they turned their backs to each other, eventually moving tight, so they were touching.

As they adjusted themselves, their backbones intertwined as if it was a zipper. As soon as that happened, although fast asleep, they found themselves in the same dream.

It was nightfall. They were holding hands, strolling along a sandy beach by the ocean. It was not a familiar scene, but it was like home. As they experienced this sense of comfort, they both glanced up at the sky, only to see two moons, full moons no less!

Suddenly, they were both butterflies, flitting about in a late spring garden. They screamed in ecstasy as they flapped their little wings and turned somersaults high in the air. Could there ever be a more joyful occasion?

As they did a butterfly hug together, Merle appeared and joined in. Now there were three beautiful butterflies!

They chased each other through the warm night sky, loving the moment they were in as they absorbed the moonlight through their wings.

They could live here in this dream forever, without another thought!

Chapter 6

The sun glowed its warming rays down on these beautiful people. It was another wonderful day as they walked to Rose's office. The door was unlocked. Inside, seated before them, a wonderful surprise. At the table was a beautiful Indian woman, smiling pleasantly.

"They call me Teesha," she said. "I found myself here this morning. I hope you don't mind."

Beth sat down beside her, taking her hand, holding it affectionately. "We have learned to be open to change, so not much surprises us. You are here, so you belong here. Welcome, Teesha."

Still in shock that she was sitting there, Mike said, "How did you get in? I saw Rose lock the door last night."

"Oh, Mike, you are such a man. Locks are for the others."

Quietly, without interrupting, Rose joined the group.

Teesha smiled uncertainly at Rose and introduced herself.

"I was out walking earlier this morning. As I walked, my mind was on how I wanted to understand my life better and be able to use my life for better purposes. Without a thought, I entered this building, found this office, and just walked in. The door was unlocked, so I sat down to wait.

I don't normally make a habit of breaking into people's offices, but I knew I belonged here."

"Not to worry, my dear. You are most welcome. Your entry proves that you are one of us, so please, sit back and stay. This explains why I brought an extra muffin and tea this morning. I was wondering.

Are you familiar with Kundalini energy, Teesha?"

"What you are doing, sounds wonderful. I am looking forward to trying it. I am only familiar with releasing it through the Third Eye, but I can understand the value of opening the connection to all Cosmic Energy. I worked with a Yogi for many years when I lived in India. They sent me here to teach others, but I feel as though I have failed because so many people are so closed to the possibilities. "

"It seems that you have found others today, Teesha. I can already feel your energy blending in with ours. Let us begin now if we are all ready. Rachel wants to speak. So please close your eyes."

Soon, everyone was clear and tuned in. The room blossomed with the fragrance of lavender, as Rachel appeared in everyone's mind.

"*Greetings all. Yes, Miss Teesha, you are in the right place. Your Yogi in India and I have long known each other. As your name implies, you are very intuitive, with great healing powers. Your special talents will find home here. You will be of great assistance in helping to raise the energy that is needed for our work.*

The human race is in metamorphosis, a state of radical change..... just like butterflies." Rachel said as she looked at Mike and Beth. "*You offer a special energy that will blend in well. Take time today to work more deeply in assimilating the new Kundalini. Once you have mastered it, there will be a whole new world for you to experience.*"

Rachel concluded, and with that, she faded from their minds.

When they had all opened their eyes and returned to earth, Rose began the day's lessons.

"I see you are integrating Merle well into your life now, Mike. This is good. I am sure that as soon as you are completely comfortable, she can join us regularly."

Not sure what she was alluding to, Mike looked down and realized that he had dressed in female clothing. He was wearing a silky red blouse over a black camisole and a knee-length black skirt.

"My mind was in a fog this morning because of our dream last night; I guess I never noticed what I put on this morning. Guess it is good that since I left the police force, I have let my hair grow longer so that I don't stand out. I have never been outside my home dressed like this before... One more step forward, eh!"

Beth gave him a big, reassuring hug and laughed, then everyone joined in.

"Let's get down to business. I am sensing that Merle may be looming nearby, so let's do a visualization process and see what happens. You will love this, Teesha.

Beth, tell us about your dream last night. That will give us a good start for our visualization."

"It was absolutely amazing! Mike and I were asleep together. Our backs were to each other when we snuggled in. As our backbones intertwined, we both projected into the same dream world!

We became butterflies. It was so delightful. So fun! "We were flitting around chasing each other, when suddenly, there were three of us. Merle had joined us.

We formed a little bouquet of pretty butterflies, then did a butterfly dance together. I just cannot describe how amazing it was, and I am so glad Merle joined in with us."

"Well, let's see if there is a dance for five butterflies."

Concentrating on their breaths, Rachel reappeared.

"*I am going to lead you in this visualization. This process is so much more than just butterflies. Butterflies are a symbol of hope and transformation.*

Begin by focusing on opening your heart chakras. We want them to become as wide as possible. Maybe you won't even be able to see or feel the edges of this chakra by the time we are there."

They fed energy into their heart centers, helping it to expand. Once it reached a certain level, they heard a pop. They each transitioned into a magnificent monarch butterfly.

When they realized what had happened, they took flight, chasing each other, playing butterfly games.

"One, two, three, four, five. Hello, Merle. Thank you for rejoining us." Merle wiggled her wings and did a little dance for everyone.

Instantly, they all began to glow even more brightly, turning a brilliant gold. Then poof! They all became one giant golden butterfly!

Together, as one, they flew quickly and gracefully with purpose. There was somewhere to go.

They could see a dense forest ahead of them. As it became clearer, they realized there were other golden butterflies, just like them. Not just a few, but thousands of golden butterflies!

As they flew into the forest, they joined right in.

It felt like home. It felt so good to be amongst others of their own kind!

As they flitted about having butterfly fun with their new friends, they all glowed brightly again. And voila! They all became another giant golden butterfly.

The process kept repeating itself over and over and over. It felt like it would never end.

After what seemed like an eternity, Rachel gradually drew each member back into their body. After some moments of reflection, they each opened their eyes to the room.

When they looked at Mike, they all laughed in joy. Merle appeared for another visit, her first visible appearance by choice, for everyone to see!

Merle smiled radiantly, looking at each person, and then slowly slipped away, becoming Mike again. Mike looked very placid. He knew what had just happened.

Merle was finally a physical reality!

The reason for all the headaches was now real. He was so overjoyed; he could not speak. He just sat and glowed.

"What a wonderful, joyful experience! I think we should all just relax for a while and enjoy the glow. See you in a while!"

With that, Rose closed her eyes and dived back into her bliss.

Mike let his mind wander as he continued to relax. He let himself think about how this power had changed his life. He had been a loner at school. The other boys liked to pick on him and call him names. Not being a big boy, he was an easy target. It seemed the other boys could smell the fear he constantly felt.

The more they bullied him, the more of a loner he became. It made no sense to him why his life seemed to be so cruel. All he wanted was peace.

Once Mike understood the power of his new gift, his life transformed. He realized the value of his new skill and became very practiced at it. His days of fear were finally over.

Without appearing to do or say anything, when they tried to torment him, the bullies unexpectedly stopped, forgetting why they approached him at all.

He just smiled at them. Eventually, they gave up and before long, they became friends.

This was a new start. He could now concentrate on his schoolwork, discovering that he actually was a very smart and talented person. The other kids got to know and enjoy the real Mike. No one was ever the wiser, or even seemed to care how or why things had shifted for him. They just embraced this loving person who was in their lives.

Mike felt really good. He was glad that he now had an opportunity to help others and give back. He smiled as he sat in the quiet. All was well.

***

Life was never the same for any of them again after that day. Even Teesha, the newcomer, had experienced the entire intense scene. Each day that followed was more like a dream than reality.

As they enjoyed the Yoga Teesha led them into, they became more familiar and stronger in their ability to manage and work with the Kundalini energy.

Finally, one day, who knows how much later, Rachel came to them in one of their visualization processes.

"*It is time now for us to begin our real work. We have all raised ourselves to an acceptable frequency that will allow us to do what we have been chosen to do. In this, you must maintain as high a level as possible from now on.*

"There are many other lessons for you to learn as we go, however, what you now can do is quite adequate for the tasks you will now begin."

Chapter 7

"Have any of you taken the time to look around this building we are in?" queried Rose.

They all looked at her, wondering where this was leading. One by one, they each answered no. They had all been so busy since they started on this project, no one had even considered looking around. However, today seemed to be the day.

Rose smiled like the cat that just caught a nice big mouse.

"This building came into my hands several years ago. It had belonged to my father. He was a real estate developer. Without knowing why, the only thing he did with this building was give it to me. Let's go have a look around."

The building was on a small street at the edge of town. It sat on several acres of flat land that had been left natural. As they walked around the building together, they noticed nothing different about it except the offices (which were all rented out) were spacious. All four floors of the building had a comfortable energy that just made people like to be here.

"When I rented to each of these businesses, it was under the condition that when I was ready to move forward, they would move out so we could have the space. My father built a new building a few blocks from here for them to move to. We will soon have the entire building... And we will need it!

Beth and Teesha, this will be the home of your main project. Mike, you will assist where needed, but, for the near future, you will have projects away from here that will need your attention.

Let's go sit outside so you can get the feel of the land we have to play with."

Once outside the back of the building, Rose led her gang along a path through the trees, leading them to a widening where an open-sided hut revealed itself before them. Inside was a large picnic table. Lunch was waiting for them.

As they ate, Rose continued explaining the plan.

"Rachel and I have been working on this plan for some time. We are going to clear some of this park so we can create some garden space and an outside healing area. Can you imagine leading some wonderful yoga sessions in this park, Teesha?"

Teesha just sat there and beamed. She knew she had found her home for now and a long future.

"We have a special friend for you to work with for developing your part of the project, Beth. She is coming down the path right now."

Beth turned to see her old friend Sheila, the child trauma therapist, approaching the hut. Beth ran to give her friend a big, welcoming hug.

After they had all welcomed Sheila, Rose continued.

"We will recreate this entire site, over the next short while, into a healing center focusing on helping children to heal themselves and to raise their energy. From them, we will create the first true generation of Homo integratis. Many of them will become our future soldiers in raising the energy of mankind.

The top floor will become sleeping rooms and living quarters for the children, the third floor will be residences for the staff while the rest of the building will become a training facility for these children and for other projects."

"The transition begins tomorrow. In the meantime, we will set the energy for our work and reaching out to our network to begin transitioning the children to our home."

"Mike, if you are wondering about your place in all this, we need you and Merle to vision our backyard. You will need to connect with the trees and plants to determine who is willing to step aside to allow space now for the garden and yoga area."

"The noble thing about our friends in the plant world is they are always connected to Source, so they will easily give themselves for a higher cause. They know that when their work is done here, they can recreate elsewhere."

***

The next morning, everyone arrived early. The excitement was so thick; it almost slowed down their walking pace. Mike headed off outside to begin his work... only to find that two sections of trees had given of themselves and died.

Surprised at the speed of the request, but not surprised by what had happened, Mike sat in the hut to connect with the family of plants in the yard. He felt Merle's presence.

Slowly and precisely, he led them into communion with the plants. As he reached optimal consciousness, the plants waved and gave off fragrant odors; they were so excited to connect with Mike and Merle.

As Mike and Merle expanded their consciousness, they embraced the essence of the plants and the earth molding into a powerful mass. Through his mind's eye, Mike could see everything around him glowing. It was as though the sun was shining from the earth.

Mike and Merle continued absorbing it into their beings when a loud thud brought them back to the outside world.

Mike looked around once he was back, and realized a tree had fallen within the group of trees that had given their lives up.

He stood up and headed off in search of the cause of the noise.

When he reached the area, he came crashing to a halt, and stared! While several enormous beavers chewed down the dying trees... several even bigger beavers were dragging the trees away!

Most of the beavers ignored Mike's presence, however, one enormous beaver that was preparing to haul a tree to their nearby pond; stood up on his hind legs, looking in Mike's direction. This beaver looked at Mike, chirped something at him in beaver language, and returned to his task.

Mike stood there, stunned, for a few moments. Just when he thought he had seen everything, the stumps left by the beavers began to disappear into the earth. Teams of gophers were pulling the stumps underground. Mike shook his head like it was an illusion... but it continued to happen! It was as if the ground was actually quicksand. The stumps just kept slipping into the earth.

Before long, the entire area of dead trees... and their stumps had vanished. The ground was ready to be cultivated. "Not a bad afternoon's work," Mike laughed to himself.

Mike returned to the gazebo, overcome by the whole situation. As he sat, closing his eyes, he gave thanks one by one to the Cosmic, the trees, the beavers, and the gophers.

Merle joined him in reconnecting with the earth energies. They focused on the beavers and the gophers, thanking them again for their help.

"I wonder if the plants are going to seed themselves." Mike pondered as he looked over the entire site. "I think we should touch base with Rose before we do any more."

***

Rose had been well immersed in her own work for the last day, so she was unaware of what had occurred. When Mike told her what had happened, she rushed down and out to the back.

She stood there staring for a few minutes, then turned, looking at him, and said, "You do have a strong connection with Mother Earth, don't you Mike! I have never seen a job done so fast and so well!

That is all of your job, for now. We want the children to be involved in the planting. Thank you for a great job done well, Mike... and Merle!

I think we need to thank the beavers and the gophers; they did all the heavy stuff." Rose laughed.

"Actually, I just thanked them," he smiled.

"Great, that puts us a couple days early at beginning your next task. We will be ready to receive the first children in about a week. Your next job is to go get them. This is going to be exciting. Our future is coming together."

"And where am I to find these children, Rose? I am sure I will not take a bus down to the mall to get them," he said, smiling at her.

"Nope, no mall, but there will be a bus. There are about thirty of them. You need to fly down south to a coastal town that is famous for being a marshaling point for children who have been kidnapped and sold into slavery. Nothing too challenging for you, I am sure."

"Great, a man's job," Mike said, followed by a quick thump in his chest. "Oh! I didn't realize Merle could hear me. Guess I had better watch myself! Who are these kids anyway?"

"Actually, they come from the same part of the world that Beth is from. That area has seen so much strife over the last century. Fighting has just become a way of life for them. These young children have not only suffered from the ravages of the war, but they have lost their parents as well. To top it off, they were all captured by some group just to sell them off like cattle.

The location where they are currently being held is just a holding pen until they are shipped off to their final destination, to become slaves. Some life!"

***

It amazed Mike at how quickly things got organized. Saying adios to everyone, he was soon sitting in the car with Beth on the way to the local airport.

"It is going to be interesting to test out my new powers and to make space for Merle to help. I can just guess this is going to be a regular pastime for me.

I can't believe how cruel and insensitive some people can become, just for the sake of money," Mike said as he and Beth worked their way through the traffic.

"Just stay alert and don't be a body hog," Beth laughed. "I heard from Rose that Merle can be quite vocal when she wants."

"She is a force to be reckoned with my dear."
As she said this, another kick bounced off his ribs.

"Ouch," he cried. "I think I know what it is like to be pregnant now!"

They both laughed... actually, all three did.

Chapter 8

It was about two hours to his destination, so Mike strategized. He poured over everything that he and Rose had discussed. It was up to him to pull all the pieces together and pull this off.

Visiting the local police station, as he arrived in the town, was first on the agenda. Updating the chief detective about his plan was not only considerate, but he almost would need their help to clean up.

Rose had given Mike the name of a local bus contractor who was willing to help him out. He would stand by at whatever time Mike needed him so they could whisk in and grab the kids.

Mike smiled to himself when he thought of them whisking in.

Entering the police station, a rather surly-looking older police officer greeted him. It was easy to tell he had seen about enough tomfoolery for one lifetime and did not seem as if he would be sympathetic to Mike's cause.

As Mike approached the officer, he smiled and made his signs discreetly. Miraculously, the officer laughed and appeared to take off about ten years of stress. When Mike asked him to direct him to the Chief Detective, the officer showed he was ready to help any way he could.

Sitting patiently, he could see the chief was busy when he arrived. The desk officer told him to hold tight. He also asked him if he wanted a drink... something that absolutely shocked the other officers around them.

And to ensure his support, he made certain there was an unobstructed view of the chief detective. Then he immediately went to work on him. He needed him to be on his side, to support him in his efforts. (Most detectives dislike foreigners coming into their space to clean up homemade messes.)

A few minutes later, the chief invited Mike into his office. The other officers stared in amazement. After all, they knew Chief to be even surlier than the desk officer. What a day this was becoming!

"How can I help you, my friend?" Chief asked with a smile. "My desk is overflowing with files needing my attention, but if this is important, I will make time for you. Just let me close the door. It seems that we are developing quite an audience."

Mike introduced himself as a retired police officer who now specializes in dealing with cold cases. He told him a bit about his history on the police force and his work for the insurance company.

Quickly, the chief recognized Mike from the news stories. "Of course! You are a legend in the world of policing. It is wonderful to meet you. I am your waiting servant, my good sir. What are you here in town for, and how may I help you?"

"Sadly, it seems there is a crime syndicate working in your fair city whose principal purpose is to kidnap children from all over the world and sell them into slavery."

"Yes, it would seem we have the misfortune of living in the perfect location for this bunch to carry on.

We have tried to figure out how they are doing it and where they are working from, but they keep eluding us," the chief replied.

"These poor kids, ya know.... all of them coming from war-torn countries. First, they killed their parents, then these guys grab them and sell them into slavery for a few measly bucks. Really bugs me we can't seem to get a handle on it."

"To help me get started, could you give me the addresses to any location you suspect they hang out or, where they might have used as a holding area? I think that will help me get a footing."

"No problem. I will personally take you to look at several sites. Gotta be careful though. They are a nasty bunch. These guys are pretty unpredictable. We would not want them to see us snooping around," Chief said as he rose from his seat, preparing to go with Mike.

"Because they do not know me, it might be better if you give me some addresses and information about them so I can be discreet. They will probably be less suspicious if I am alone. Besides, I have taken up enough of your day already.

I will keep you apprised as things develop if that is okay with you. I appreciate your hospitality, but I realize you are a busy person."

***

Why is it bad guys always work the night shift? This meant working late into the night himself to get this situation wrapped up. Mike checked into the hotel room Rose had reserved for him. It was a perfect place for him to move about without being noticed. Mike took his time having dinner and freshening up, preparing himself for the evening ahead.

The first task was to relax and connect with Merle. She would undoubtedly have some input on how to best handle this. Within seconds, Merle burst out. These guys were going down if she would help it.

She dressed in a very sexy royal blue velvet pantsuit that would draw the attention of any warm-blooded man. Her focus, however, was only one small group that needed to reconsider their career choices.

Mike had rented a car, so she slipped out the back way and headed off to survey the sites the chief had listed for them. When she arrived in the part of town where all the locations seemed to be, she stopped the car and took the list out of her pocket.

She stared at the list for a moment, then laid it down flat, whereby she ran her hand over the page. It only had one address left on it.

Her first job was preparing for the upcoming intervention. She called the bus contractor, introducing herself as Mike's assistant. She relayed to him the instructions to bring the bus down to a location near, but not in view of the lone address, so he could be ready when needed.

The next call was to the chief to have him prepared to raid the establishment once she had found the children.

Heading off in search of the right address, Merle accessed her own GPS, the most efficient way to find one's way. She laughed to herself.

Thirty minutes later, she had found it. It was an old restaurant inside a seedy-looking building near the docks.

"Couldn't be a more obvious place, I mean really guys," she laughed to herself.

She parked right across from the restaurant, making sure the occupants noticed her. As she sat, she watched the activity inside the building. She sat there for about ten minutes when two tough-looking men walked out of the building, heading straight toward her.

And as they approached, she stepped out of the car, leaning against it in a very provocative pose.

The men changed their energy from 'We'll show you' to 'Huhabubba, baby, let me show you the world!'

It pleased her that she was already so comfortable with her skills. The men became putty in her hands. She said she was looking for some real men. Ones who could help her on her mission, and she did not want big talkers. She had a project that needed a lot of soldiers to pull it off that could be worth mucho denaros.

They suggested she should join them in the restaurant since their boss was in the cafe that night. He was the man to lead her army; they said. She followed them in, surveying everything about the location.

Immediately, seeing her enter their den, the boss jumped to his feet and yelled at the two men who had invited her in. They knew they were under strict orders to keep anyone, not a member, out and to use any method necessary to keep the rule.

Merle looked at the boss as she entered the cafe and smiled. He melted and sat down again, offering her the seat of a man sitting close to him.

"What can I do for you, my dear? My world is yours." he stared at her.

Her hand moving ever so discreetly, setting the energy for the shift, she continued smiling.

"Oh, I just came to collect all the children you have kidnapped and to put you out of business," Merle stated nonchalantly as she stared at the boss.

Every man in the restaurant sat down in their chair. The boss smiled and sighed as he joined them.

"Where are the children, right now?" she asked. The boss pointed to a door to the rear of the restaurant as he sagged into his chair.

It was unlocked, so once through, she followed a long hallway and headed down a set of stairs to another door. This door was locked. She smiled her smile and turned the knob. It was no problem for her.

Inside the room were the children.

Mission complete, Merle called the police chief, telling him to move his men in, then called the bus driver to position the bus near the restaurant.

Less than two minutes later, the site was overrun with uniformed police officers. It astonished them when they walked in. All the men sitting on chairs, waiting to be arrested.

The boss looked at the chief and said, "We were waiting for you. We have decided to change our ways."

Chief stared at the man, not sure whether to believe him when suddenly the door at the rear opened up. Out came Merle with thirty children in tow!

Chapter 9

As Mike walked up the path to the 'Matrix', the girls came rushing out to meet him. After all the hugs and greetings, Beth led him around to the back.

Mike reveled at the new statue in the yard near the first garden. It was a giant golden butterfly carved out of wood. It appeared weatherworn, and yet, according to Beth, it found itself there sometime yesterday.

"We arrived here yesterday morning, to prepare for the arrival of the children when I stepped into the yard for a breath of fresh air. That is when I saw it standing there as if it had always been there." Beth laughed. "Miracles never cease around here, do they!"

After Beth had called everyone to see their recent addition but found out nothing about how it came to be there, Mike felt some giggling inside himself... giggling like a schoolgirl who had hidden her friend's lunch!

"I think I know the answer," Mike said as he transformed into Merle.

"I thought it would be nice to have a constant reminder of that wonderful visualization we did, so, I manifested it. A budding artist now too, if I have to say so myself."

The rescued children were due in about two days, once the authorities had cleared them. Preparing all the tasks for their homecoming had a tight timeline. In fact, some of the staff were preparing parts of the children's first meal in their new home.

The officer from the Immigration department called Rose to update her on their progress.

"We have investigated the lives of each of the children, in an attempt to reconnect them with their parents. All of the thirty children collected are in the same age group, 8-10. It is our determination they still need the parents they were born to. However, failing that, we will be releasing each of the children who we feel are orphaned to your organization.

So far, we have been able to only reconnect six children with their parents. We feel many of the parents have chosen to let them go, as they know having them return to the ongoing situation will not help them. A huge sacrifice, I am sure."

The most important job right now was preparing for the integration process. These kids had been through a lot; a lot more than any person should ever suffer through in their whole lives, never mind their quick sprint.

With Sheila and Beth leading the way, Rose knew she had the right staff.

"We are already looking at expanding our facility," Rose said. "With thirty children soon to arrive, we are near capacity... and Mike... we have received notice of another project for you. Another group of children will be waiting to be rescued soon. However, we have to wait for the situation to conclude first, so maybe you can help around here for now. You know, in your special way."

***

Mike headed off for a wander in their park to settle himself down. He enjoyed being recognized, but, at heart, he desired no praise.

***

Finally alone, Mike started relaxing and being one with himself, walking and communing with nature, his best friend. He surveyed the work of the beavers and gophers. His thoughts wandered to a subject that seemed to be on his mind a lot; how humans and nature might work together, if only man could get his ego out of the way.

Once the animals had everything cleaned up; who was to know trees had ever lived there?

Mike stooped down and pushed his hand into the soil, letting the energy flow into him. "The soil is not ready for gardening yet. Better give it some time to breathe before we start."

With that he visualized the soil being rototilled gently to break up the surface, making it easier to work. No longer surprised, Mike opened his eyes to see millions of earthworms busy preparing the soil. As fast as he spoke the words, they were done in both gardens and returned to the depths of the soil.

"This is really fun... And labor-saving. Sure beats. the old way of doing things!"

Speaking of the way things get done; Mike discovered that Merle had been busy too.

Without needing to be visible, Merle had manifested a long wing addition added onto the Matrix. The formerly square-looking building now was

L-shaped. He wondered if that was the job that Rose had mentioned. Time to go find out!

Chapter 10

Back inside the Matrix, the girls had not seen the changes outside; because they had been so busy with their own work. Mike laughed to himself, choosing to let them find them on their own.

"Oh Mike, you are here now. Good. Let's get started on your special job if you are ready," Rose said to him. "You are looking especially proud of yourself. What have you been up to?"

"You will find out soon enough! I am enjoying myself. What would you like me to do?"

"These kids need a safe and comfortable place to cocoon. I would like you to scan all the staff to ensure everyone is on board with us. After you have finished, I would like you to set the energy, so the children will feel safe."

Mike found a quiet place to observe the staff as they worked. Indiscretions had no place in this project. Everyone had to be there, completely committed.

***

Settling himself in a corner, but near where the staff were preparing the schoolroom, he watched the activity going on.

There was a good mix of people. They all seemed happy and motivated.

Mike closed his eyes, visualizing gold energy filling all the space. As an important extra, he included a layer of truth energy to cause each person to show their true self.

He took a deep breath and blew it out to fill the room. As he opened his eyes again to check the activities in front of him, he saw each person become more relaxed and joyful.

He then moved to the kitchen. It was humming as people prepared food. Mike was glad there would soon also be a good meal for everyone here now. This work made him really hungry.

He found a discreet spot and repeated the earlier process. When he opened his eyes, he found again the same result, except that a young man had slumped down, sobbing.

Knowing others would look after this man, he petitioned Rose to intervene. Magically, she appeared within seconds and walked right to the crying man.

She sat down, taking his hand, being careful not to overwhelm him. He grasped her hand so tight it became uncomfortable, but he was unable to look at her.

Rose waited for him to reveal himself. She looked over at Mike and prompted him to focus on him.

The young man, feeling the shift, mumbled, "I need help. I don't understand what is happening to me. I need help!"

Rose assured him. "You are safe here, Tomas. When you are ready, you can tell me what you don't understand. I am here to help you."

Soon Tomas began convulsing. He fell to the floor, unconscious.

Mike continued, focusing on Tomas. He knew he was okay, but there was something big he needed to shift. In a second, Tomas visibly transformed into female form.

She sat up and looked around, remaining quiet for a few moments trying to orient herself; then looked straight at Rose.

"Finally," she laughed. "I have been trying to get his attention for the longest time. I have work to do too. I can't do it when he is in the way."

Mike shifted on the spot, becoming Merle, and sat down beside her, taking her hand gently.

"Welcome. You are among friends." Merle said quietly, but barely able to hold back her excitement.

"I am Tarita. I tried to join you when you were playing butterflies, but Tomas does not know how to let me out." She paused, sighing. "I do not want to go back to him. I want to be free."

Ever watchful, Rachel appeared before them. She smiled at Tarita, saying, "*I understand how you feel, my little butterfly. However, to gain true freedom, one must become all they truly are. To deny part of yourself is to limit yourself and your capabilities.*"

She stopped for a moment to let her message be soaked in by everyone, but meant it for Tarita. She continued, "*Tomas means twin. He is your male aspect. You were born into a male body... for a particular reason. It is your destiny to live primarily in a male body, at this time.*" Again, she stopped to allow Tarita to absorb her message.

"But why do I need him? I can do so much better without him."

"*Your lesson is to learn to love your male side and to learn to work through him. As twins, you have a special connection that serves in a way other people cannot enjoy.*

It appears there will be more for you to embrace as you grow, as names often imply aspects of your life purpose. You have a special name, Tarita... Butterfly. We want to help you fly in all your glory."

Rachel turned to Merle but spoke again to Tarita. "*This is Merle. She is like you. Her male aspect I call Michael, after the Archangel. Merle and Michael will teach you how to live as your true self. You can only truly love at all if you can love yourself in all manner.*"

Rachel blessed everyone as she faded away. Merle smiled at Tarita, offering her a hand to pull her up to standing. Reluctantly, Tarita complied and soon found herself pulled into a big hug. Merle now had a little sister... and, I guess you would say Mike got a little brother... all in one!

They walked down to the next floor and found an unoccupied Yoga room. Merle guided Tarita over to an available mat on the floor and sat them down, going into Lotus position. Facing each other, Merle took both of Tarita's hands in hers, locking eyes with her.

Merle said nothing as she processed energy with her, helping her to relax and let go of her fears. Then Tarita became Tomas again. And a few minutes later, she popped out again. It kept happening again and again until, finally, Tarita started laughing and laughing.

Merle repeated the same process flowing between herself and Mike so Tomas and Tarita knew they were not alone.

"I get it now," Tarita laughed. "It seems different when I am Tomas, but it is okay."

Tomas again reappeared.

"There are many of us who can shift between our integrated male and female aspects. We can do this because we have special jobs that require being able to work in either gender. You will now begin learning how to work with this ability, but first, we need to find out what your purpose is." Merle whispered.

Merle asked Tarita to sit while she prepared a concoction they called Destiny Tea.

"This is a powerful drink that will take you into your higher self. You will visit yourself in the distant future, so you can look back and see the path that will support your greatest progress as a soul. There will be specific events along the way, that are key to providing you with the opportunity to grow and become the ultimate dynamic person you are capable of becoming. I will sit by to support you through the process."

Merle handed her the tea and sat on a couch nearby. Tarita downed the tea and closed her eyes. As she drifted off, Merle connected with her to witness her process.

Tarita focused on her breath. Relaxing her mind, she connected with her physical body. It became like she was a liquid in a long tube, flowing to an unknown destiny.

For a period that seemed like forever, she sat limp, smiling a serene smile, as if she was enjoying a really pleasant movie.

Soon she saw a nice, inviting yellow light. The light became more and more intense as she flowed along the tube until it solidified into a form. When the form became visible, Tarita became still. The light then immersed itself in her and they became one.

Tarita looked back and saw her destiny!   A Golden Butterfly!

Chapter 11

Mike and Tomas were well entrenched in the plan for retrieving the next group of children. It was more complicated than the last one, as it required infiltrating a country that restricts access to foreigners.

Mike wanted to make sure that Tomas had instilled enough confidence in himself to transition into Tarita as required... and to think on his or her feet.

Mike thought it would be helpful if Tomas tried out a little homegrown trouble, just to see how he handled it.

A local motorcycle gang had built a business, forcing local business owners to pay them a fee to ensure their safe passage. A few owners had refused and paid the cost, finding their businesses burned down for some inexplicable reason.

Mike had helped Tomas to learn and use his energy technique so he could shift their consciousness; however, Tomas was new at it, unlike Mike, to whom it was now second nature. No time like now to find out how well he had it ingrained!

***

Tomas had no biker genes like his friend, so he had to create a whole other persona that would get their attention. This would take some serious detail.

The biker gang hung out at a local bar. The owner had involuntarily become an associate of the gang, and was now providing free drinks and food to keep the boys from busting up his business.

Mike found out where the bar owner lived, so he could speak with him away from the eyes of the bikers. When he knocked on the door of the man's house, he was greeted by a slight man who looked much older than he really was. He had suffered more than enough for one lifetime. It was obvious, he needed help.

"I will do anything to get rid of these guys, but am so scared, so I just do whatever they want. I am going broke providing them with their beer and food. Soon my suppliers will cut me off.... then what?" The barkeep said.

"My associate will come work for you as a waiter. Need to toughen him up a bit, so I want him to work around these guys for a while before we bring them down. What kind of window do we have before you cannot supply them?"

"Wow, maybe a couple of weeks, tops. I am not sure if I have the guts to pull this off. There will literally be hell to pay if they get wind."

Mike then explained he was an intuitive who trained people how to live in their power. If he would accept it, Mike would do a process on him to both bring up his power and to give him the quiet confidence to stay safe and play his part. Not sure what he was getting himself into, the barkeep agreed.

Although it was nighttime, Mike led the man into a park nearby so that he could use the energy of the forest to help him. At first, the man was reluctant to follow him, but Mike just smiled walking into the park.

"Sit down here and relax. Lean against this amazing cedar tree. See if you can smell its fragrance."

Mike sat across from him and closed his eyes. He started projecting golden light at the man. Mike could feel him relax and accept the light. His energy became much bigger and stronger.

"I never realized how strong the smell of these trees is. I love it!" he said.

They both opened their eyes and sat without moving for a few minutes. Mike connected with him to check how he was now feeling. He needed the man's confidence in Mike and Tomas, so they could succeed with pulling off this project without a hitch.

***

The next afternoon, Tomas began his new career as a bar waiter. Not knowing that Mike was watching him telepathically, Tomas began cleaning tables and getting the bar ready for the day. Soon, the bikers rolled in, making their typical fanfare of showing off as they pulled up.

The first biker to arrive noticed Tomas working as he came in, and called the gang leader to inform him of the intruder. He then sat down in the corner, demanded a beer, and sat observing Tomas.

Tomas had never dealt with people like the bikers before, so was quite nervous as he worked, but he raised his energy, becoming confident and detached in front of his observer.

Not much later, the gang leader walked in. He was a big man who towered over everyone. His scruffy-looking appearance was intimidating, Obviously, being fashionable and clean were not requirements for leading this group of thugs. As soon as he saw Tomas, he searched for the owner.

"What's the deal with the new guy? I did not say you could hire anyone. I guess you can afford to pay me more if you can afford to hire help, eh!" the leader growled.

"He is my nephew. I am feeling off, so, so he offered to help me… until I feel better. He will not be a problem. I…I have no more money to give you. I am almost bankrupt now."

"I guess soon I will be the owner, and you can be the waiter. Think I will buy you a little costume to wear to celebrate your promotion!" The leader laughed as he turned to sit with the other members.

"Hey waiter, bring me and the boys something good to eat and some more beer, pronto! I want to see what kind of lacky you are... or do I have to train you myself?" he sneered.

Tomas almost ran into the kitchen to join the owner. This guy made him so nervous. He stopped for a moment to focus on his breath. He needed to maintain his power if he was going to pull this off. Right now, he felt like he could just head for the back door and keep running forever.

Focusing on his breath for a moment, he felt his power rise again. He then projected energy to the owner to help him stay up.

"How long have you been putting up with this? I am having trouble with only a few minutes of these guys."

"Six months, seven days a week," he replied. "He is not usually this gruff. I think he is just showing off for your benefit, so walk slow with a big stick, as they say!"

***

By the end of the first day, Tomas felt like he had run a marathon. The bikers, who often took off for a few hours to do their business, never left for the entire day. They tormented Tomas in every way they could think of. Tomas held his own, never cracking his resolve or doing anything that might up the ante with these people.

Upon his return to the Matrix, he sought Mike out for a discussion.

"I have never felt such negative energy in my whole life, Mike. I had to stop several times during the day to recharge myself, but I made it!" Tomas laughed as his nerves betrayed his confidence.

"I told you it was going to be a challenge for you," Mike laughed. "This is excellent training. Future projects will not be this easy. Just keep remembering the kids we are going to help, so you can keep focused."

All at once, Tomas went quiet and closed his eyes. Tarita then appeared. She looked angry. As she started to say something, Mike put up his hand to silence her. He then closed his eyes, allowing Merle to appear.

Tarita looked at Merle. "I just want to destroy these guys. Who do they think they are? What are we waiting for?" She raised her hand to deflect the energy, smiling at her new friend. It became apparent she also needed training on managing her emotions and her power.

"This is a big lesson for you, too, Tarita. To truly be the magnificent person you have the potential to be, you need to master your mind and your emotions. Recognize how you feel right now and lock it into your memory. Every time you start to feel this way, you need to transition this energy into good, positive energy. You are a powerful person with amazing skills, but until you learn to master yourself, you cannot begin to follow your destiny." As Merle concluded this, she closed her eyes and focused on her breath.

Tarita realized the truth in what Merle had told her and resolved to master herself. Becoming her true butterfly was all she dreamed of. Now was her chance.

***

For the next few days, Tomas kept to himself as he worked. The bikers continued to harass him. He remained resolute that he would keep his power, no matter what. Tomas could tell that things were getting out of hand. The bikers counted on breaking Tomas and would do anything to ensure their superiority.

About a week later, Tomas met with Mike to discuss his concerns.

"I am concerned that they are going to hurt one of us soon. I think Tarita and I have had enough lessons here. Let's do something before there is irreparable damage."

They had come a long way over the past week. Mike decided that this had gone on long enough, too. He then went to visit the barkeep.

"Stay home tomorrow. I am going to go to work at your place. It is time to transition this situation," he told him. The barkeep was resistant, as he knew the cost of not showing up, but he trusted Mike.

***

The next day when the gang arrived, it was very apparent that today was the right day to bring this episode to an end. As they entered, the anger in the air was so thick, one could almost eat it.

"Who are you?" the leader spat at Mike. "Why are you here? Do I have to approve of you now too?"

Mike and Tomas continued with their work, ignoring the leader. They wanted to ensure that all the members were present before they did anything.

"I am talking to you!" the leader roared at Mike. He slapped a baseball bat on the counter behind Mike. He slapped it again when Mike did not even flinch.

The bar was visible as he looked in the mirror. Tomas had told him how many members were there on a regular day. He concentrated on making himself look busy cleaning the counter as he counted heads. They were all here.

Mike turned to Tomas, who was watching him from the corner of his eye. When Mike raised his hand to make the symbol, Tomas mirrored him.

The bar went quiet.

Chapter 12

Everyone was excited to hear the story about how Mike and Tomas had taken down the motorcycle gang. Mike was being vague about what had gone on. He wanted the real hero to share the story of the triumph after they finished dinner.

Finally, they cleared the tables. Rose invited Mike to stand up and share.

"I am going to step aside and let the person who genuinely deserves to tell the story of this event speak," as he turned to Tomas. "You have come into your own now, my friend. You may not have known it, but when I raised my arm... that was all I did... you stopped the Banditos. Your projecting the gold energy shifted their minds. I raise my glass to you, Tomas."

The news stunned him. The entire table erupted with applause, and then they started chanting "Tomas, Tomas, Tomas!"

Tomas pulled himself together long enough to stand up and tell the story. He just glowed with confidence. A new person stood before them. The old, timid Tomas was forever gone.

***

The next morning, when they reconvened, Rose told them that Rachel wanted to speak to them this morning, so they all relaxed and closed their eyes. Within minutes, everyone was in the zone and Rachel was beaming her ever-famous smile at each of them.

"*We are truly progressing well on our journey to enlightenment and Grace. The occurrences of late have shown us we have chosen the best people for the job. When I last spoke with Tarita, she was having difficulty with understanding why she needed to be embodied in a male body.*"

She then turned, looking at Tomas. "*You have proven yourself, my dear Thomas. I trust that the light within you burns much brighter now.*"

As she spoke to Tomas, he reframed into Tarita. "Sorry to interrupt, Rachel. I want to tell you it has made me so happy and excited about what happened. All of my anxieties about being limited by Tomas have vanished!"

"*It is essential that all human beings, whether Homo Sapiens or Homo integratis, understand that* true personal power can only be achieved through their interactions with others.

One solitary person carries no genuine power. They are limited by their own singular understanding, whereas two souls in harmony can achieve anything. Mike and Tomas, or Merle and Tarita are embodiments of a fortunate gift. Carrying the power of two within them at all times, there is no need to search for their perfect partner."

Rachel then turned to Beth. "That takes away nothing of what you have with Michael, Bethany. It is through your love that all we have today is possible. It is the power of exponentials.

From the time of birth, we believe our goal is to find love. The truth is that love is with us at all times. Love is inherent in our nature. It is just a matter of how we understand love. When we mature to where we can love others and give them the power to love themselves, without giving our own power away, we truly have mastered love... and life."

Rachel gave her sign of blessing and then faded away.

Everyone remained still for a very long time. They rested, contemplating the message Rachel had spoken.

***

The children were to arrive today, all twenty four of them at once. There had been plenty of time for preparation. They knew they had done their best, so they were confident everything would go well. These children had suffered a lot already, so everyone wanted to ensure that they would fall in love with The Matrix as soon as they arrived.

Not long after the meeting closed, they heard the sounds of a bus parking. They all headed for the front of the building. As the children stepped off the bus, a group of smiling adults welcomed them.

Some children were fearful about their future, living with this group of unusual, unfamiliar adults. They had never known adults they could trust or feel comfortable with during their entire lives. This would be a big challenge for them.

Sheila, Teesha, and Beth signaled to the children to follow them. They formed a parade into the building ... and right back out again... into the garden at the rear.

Outside, the staff had set up blankets all over the grassy area, and on several tables lay a big smorgasbord of yummy dishes and healthy drinks. The children stopped and stared; they could not believe their eyes. There were green salads, chicken burgers, hot dogs, raw veggies, and freshly picked fruits. A veritable feast of delicious organic foods.

Beth moved over to the buffet, waving her hand for them to dig in. Slowly, the children approached, expecting the worst, but after one brave girl took a plate, helping herself to salads and fruit and smokies, the food found its purpose.

They had been used to poor food and starvation. The government agency that quarantined them at their intake center fed them well but it was institutional food. They were hungry for some good wholesome homemade food.

It was easy to tell by the looks on their faces how they were overjoyed as they tasted the yummy food and, of course, plenty of different yummy juices to quench their thirst.

When their plates were full, they sat themselves down on the blankets to enjoy their meal. They sat in groups based on what language they spoke. They all chatted quietly, looking down at the food, sometimes sharing one of their morsels with another.

This arrangement was helpful, as Rose needed to know what language each child spoke. There were several. Fortunately, the folks at the intake center had briefed them regarding what languages the children spoke. This allowed Rose to ensure that there were staff present that spoke their language. Beth took charge of this part of the intake, as she understood a couple of the dialects, even though she had not spoken them since childhood.

As the meal wrapped up, the staff members who spoke the other languages approached their group. They called the children to order and introduced themselves and the center.

The expressions on the children's faces varied. Some were excited about finally having a home, while some did not know what to make of it all. Many were definitely not trusting anyone, even after good food.

The staff could remedy the ill feelings, but they opted not to. They felt the children had the right to feel their emotions. It also allowed the therapy staff, who were all watching them, to determine the mental state of each child without them realizing they were being watched.

After the introductions, there was a special surprise... hundreds of beautiful butterflies floated down from the trees. At first, they stayed well above the children, doing little dances in the air. The children watched in awe, smiling and giggling at the beautiful sight.

As the children became more comfortable with the show, the butterflies fluttered down into their reach. Some even landed on their arms. The show was a success.

Rose looked proudly at Tarita, beaming over the success of her contribution to the children's first day in their new home.

***

The next task was to introduce the children to their new home. After this wondrous show, they were excited to go exploring.

The children came with no extra clothes or supplies, so they had nothing to carry up to their living quarters. They were all eager to see where their rooms were, however, so they changed the plans to finding their new nests.

They could pick their own beds and roommates. The children were quite young, so the staff did not separate the boys from the girls, however, the children did. It worked out perfectly. Billeting themselves by gender and language into the beds and rooms, leaving no one out.

The children showed no interest in the remainder of the building. They were weary travelers. Realizing their desire for some shuteye, the staff showed them where the toilets and wash facilities were and left them alone to rest for a while.

***

Later in the afternoon, when the children felt refreshed, the staff showed them into one of the large rooms on the floor below the living quarters. They could not believe their eyes when they walked into the room. Rows of tables with new clothes lay stacked on each one. No uniforms like one would expect, but regular clothes that young pre-teen children would wear.

They had set the room up, girls on the one side, boys on the other. Gravitating to their side of the room, they searched for some new clothes for themselves. It was fun finding new outfits and showing them off.

When done, they brought their old clothing to the room after changing, placing them in boxes to be taken to a site and burned. That part of their lives was over, never to be replayed.

By the evening, twenty four sets of little eyelids were heavy and ready to close. They all went quietly to their beds after they were each issued soaps and toothbrushes. (Several did not even know how to brush their teeth!)

They were all ready for a good sleep, and a new day tomorrow.... and a new life.

They could not know how wonderful their new life would become. Only time would tell.

Chapter 13

Once the children had settled in, the real work began. Rachel was waiting to speak with the staff when the sun broke in the morning. There was no time to waste in getting these children repaired.

"Good morning to all of you. I am called Rachel. I am charged with the responsibility of ensuring the Matrix project is carried out to the highest level, now and for always. I felt it necessary to speak to everyone today, as each of you must understand the importance of your role in this project. There is no one here that is just staff, so please keep in mind that how you take part here affects not only you, but the other members of the staff... and... the children.

Every one of you has been given the freedom to grow as souls, to face your own special challenges while building on your own strengths. You are invited to take part in any of the activities we offer, including working with any of the counselors.

As you already know, this is a unique project. It is unlike any other activity you have considered before. Please be open to giving and receiving as situations develop. Your strength and power will increase immeasurably when you do.

These children are very special. Special, because they have been through so much in their young lives. Their suffering, though; has provided them with a special opportunity to develop into soldiers of life, since the trauma they have encountered has torn open their minds in a way that is not likely to be experienced in a normal childhood.

Our job is to help them heal and to use their ability to access the deepest regions of their being to become powerful forces for good, here on Mother Earth.

With this, I leave you in capable hands... yours."

***

As Rachel faded away, excitement and conversation filled the air. Everyone was ready to start a new day... and a very special life.

As the people in the room filtered out, heading for the cafeteria, Rose gave sheets of paper to each staff member, outlining their duties for the day.

***

After breakfast and a rest, the children headed to one of the large open rooms on the next floor down. As they entered, they saw mats placed in several rows. At one end of the room, was Teesha.

The children were starting today (and every day thereafter) with yoga. As Rose and the others looked on, Teesha glanced over to them with the biggest smile possible. She had found her home.

Teesha led them in some simple stretching exercises at first. With the exercises, she encouraged laughter as they tried this strange new activity. As an experienced yoga master, she understood the value of laughter in the healing process. This was a key component in helping their bodies accept these new and unknown movements to replace the ones learned through the fears of days past.

As they advanced into more serious moves, she taught them how to breathe correctly by moving their tummy muscles. She also introduced them to quiet time, so they could learn to be comfortable in their body.

After over an hour of playing yoga, they were ready for some refreshments and some fresh air, so everyone headed outside to the back. The staff had already set up a table with snacks and fruit juice. It was gone in a flash. Sandwiches and pastries were gobbled down as fast as little hands could grab them.

As they savored the break, some kids wandered off to explore the territory. A couple of boys even strayed as far as the beaver ponds but came scurrying back when mama beaver saw them trying to climb on her house.

Rose smiled proudly as she noted the children were now mixing more. Even though they could not speak with each other, they spoke by using their hands and body gestures. The light bulb went on.

She returned to her office and grabbed her phone book.

"Hi, Magda, how busy are you these days? I have a great idea for you. Can you come to my office sometime today?"

Magda presented herself not long after. "What is up, my friend? I have not heard from you in a long time. What have you got going on here? This building is looking very different since the last time I was here."

Rose explained about the new project. She then told her about what had developed with the children. and wanted to know if she was still teaching Sign Language.

"I have not been working for a while now. The school I was at ended the program. I was considering relocating somewhere else, but now, I assume, I have discovered a fresh audience.

I have been wanting to help youths to expand their own understanding of themselves through learning to communicate using only gesturing or Sign language, as we call it.

I think it will help them understand communication better, because they will come to understand that much of what we speak is done through our body. I think there is a positive incentive for them to pick it up quickly as they are already trying to speak to others who cannot express with them verbally. When can I start, Rose?"

Rose introduced her friend Magda to the other staff. Giving resounding approval to the idea,, they voted to introduce this new offering right away as a follow-up to yoga.

Not one to waste time, Rose led her gang into where the children were waiting. She called the translators over to explain what was about to occur. Then each of them called their group together to explain.

Within 15 minutes, Magda had the children all signing to each other.

The staff were all amazed at how willing and receptive these young people were. It was almost like they had always been right here. They were all so hungry to learn.

Everyone knew that some challenging times lay ahead. All this start-up energy had not taken away the fears, terror, or hardship that any of these little people had been put through in their previous life.

For right now, these children were learning just to be kids.

***

It was not long before the children showed signs they needed to engage the de-stressing programming. Some of them had wet their beds, while some picked fights with other children as an outlet to vent the anger entrenched inside their little bodies.

Sheila and Beth were ready to implement their plan. They knew deep trauma issues could be difficult to change, needing many years of counseling and treatment.

That the children did not speak English well added to the problem. However, it helped that they were youngsters, still open to change. Willingness to engage made everything easier.

***

Standard detraumatizing processes can take years to have lasting effects. There was no time for years. The success of this project depended on a smooth transition that was safe, quick, and beneficial to the child for the short, long term, and permanent.

For this to happen, it needed to be done on the spiritual level, a special clearing process. This would require assistance from Rachel.

The children moved into the yoga room. It was the afternoon of another busy day for them. The staff had pushed them hard today to wear them out. They had learned and practiced new yoga moves, practiced conversing in sign language while they played games, and had enjoyed a yummy picnic outside.

During their outside time, the staff had a special treat for them... screaming!

The staff felt they had spent so much time not talking this day that they should discharge all that unspent talking in a fun way. It is especially frustrating trying to speak with one's hands and body when they were trained from birth to communicate with their voice.

The children followed Sheila into the middle of the forest, where she began making funny sounds. She smiled at the children as she did it. Beth and Tarita joined in and soon everyone was kibitzing, imitating the movements of the animals as they let themselves go. Some sounded like monkeys, while others squawked like birds, or made weird noises. They were all having fun, releasing the stress in their bellies.

Once they had filed back to the yoga room, the staff served them a very special tea created under the watchful eye of Rachel. They rested on the floor mats. One by one, they settled back and dozed off.

As they relaxed, the staff sat nearby and went into meditation, allowing Rachel to appear. She surveyed the children. All was well. She gestured to Tarita.

Tarita expanded her energy, repeating her deep breathing until it filled the entire room. Then, visualizing herself as a beautiful golden butterfly, she took flight.

Into the consciousness of each child she flew, flitting about as she sprinkled gold dust into the air, seeping down into their energy fields. Many children giggled as they slept.

As Tarita plied her magic powder, Rachel swept their minds clear with a whisper of a wind that blew away their fears. They floated free. Something they had never known before. The true healing process had now begun.

The children lay there for a long time. It was close to nightfall when they woke. They gave each child an enormous piece of special cake when they returned to the room. The cake would help them feel full, grounding them after such a long trip out of their body.

A while later, their smiling faces all lit up, they were ready for one more special treat. Donning jackets and toques the staff supplied, they returned to the outdoors. Once they reached the area that Mike and his friends had cleared earlier in the year, Sheila invited them to look up into the sky.

The night sky was crystal clear. Gazing up in awe, they watched the movie unfold before them; the moon rose, the stars twinkled while the planets stood guard over their sky.

Beth pointed out various celestial bodies, but the best part was the constellations.

"That one over there, where you see the three stars in a straight line, that is Orion's belt. If you look long enough, you will see him completely, perching there above us, watching over us from his heavenly nest. Orion's job is to keep us safe while we travel at night. He will constantly be there for us every night as we move through our lives, sending his love down.

Over there is the Big Dipper. Keep an eye on it occasionally as we watch the show. You will see the long spoon move in its rotation. The Big Dipper is part of the constellation called Ursa Major, or Big Bear.

The Big Dipper pivots around the North Star. The ancients used it to guide them as they traveled at night."

The highlight of the show for this gathering under the stars soon appeared clearly before them- The Pleiades.

"Legends abounded in ancient circles about the Pleiades", she told them. "This constellation is the home to the universe's wise folk who gather to steer the course of all that lives. This is the land where God's highest servants, the true Masters of Creation, reside when they are resting and preparing to create the future.

***

Everyone was pretty tired the following morning, but every person was wide awake at breakfast. The children seemed to be mesmerized by last night's event. It was a good starting point for them, as the big shift would happen today, likely for all of them.

The adults positioned themselves around the room so they could observe the children. Even after such a late evening, the kids still wanted to do yoga and signing.

Sharing the burden of creating the day's schedule with the children was vital to their work. It gave them a sense of self-empowerment, by letting them choose for themselves what the day would look like, so Rose relented, rescheduling the meditation until later.

As they came into the room, they sat on their yoga mat and remained quiet until Rose turned to them and spoke. "How many of you are still feeling anxious in your tummy?" she asked. "Do any of you have any other discomfort in your body?"

They each raised their hands at the first question, but the second was the vital one. Several boys raised their hands, and when questioned by the translator, they each replied that they felt like someone was kicking them from the inside.

Rose nodded to the team leaders to make a note of who they were.

"The process for this session will support you in releasing the bad feelings you have inside yourself. Our goal is to support you in feeling calm and peaceful. It will also help you get to appreciate and accept yourself more fully."

As she finished, a staffer played a special tune on a Pan flute.

It only took a moment for everybody to settle down, promptly closing their eyes as they stretched back on their mat. Even some staff joined them as the hypnotic melodies overcame them.

Once everybody was in the perfect state, Rose closed her eyes, then Rachel appeared.

She said nothing at first, then overflowed the room with a golden energy that sloshed back and forth over everyone, like the tide in the ocean. As each wave rolled over the crowd; they released old restricting beliefs, freeing them to develop into more amazing individuals. The tide kept washing back and forth, back and forth, until they were all sparkling clean.

After completing this exercise, she surveyed everyone to measure the level of release they had attained.

Tarita filled the entire room with white energy. As they absorbed it, it expelled the stagnant energy held by old dysfunctional beliefs. That repugnant energy was whisked off into the Universe.

They could see the difference in how each child relaxed. Now, they were ready to assume their personal power, they would soon meet their own personal destiny.

Chapter 14

Rachel left specific instructions with the team regarding the next steps to be taken. The children needed to be separated according to their specific needs.

Many of the children were Homo Sapiens, therefore limited in their potential for this lifetime. To make space for processing more children that Mike's team would rescue, they would need to be adopted out. Fortunately, the city they lived in had many young families.

The first thing that was needed was an adoption process that would support the children to continue maturing. They had all suffered way more than any child ever should; therefore, the team had to ensure that they were placed in loving, supportive homes so the training they received at the Matrix could continue to grow with them.

They then instituted a program where local families were invited to meet the children. Each child could decide if they wished to be adopted out or if they would stay inside the Matrix. Even if they left, they would still take part with their families in Matrix programs.

They posted notices around town and in the local newspaper, telling people about the opportunity to adopt a child. It did not take long for the lineup to begin.

The staff researched each family, interviewing them to make sure they were suitable... and willing to continue the work of the Matrix staff. This was an opportunity for each of them to grow as well. After all, true growth can only continue significantly in a nurturing environment such as a healthy family.

Soon, over half of the children had chosen their new families. What a joyous event!

Some children who were siblings even got to join families where they could continue fostering and enjoying this special relationship.

They truly felt inside they needed and wanted to be part of a family with a Mom and a Dad who loved and supported them... just like regular kids!

None of the boys who had felt the kicking inside of them opted to join a family. They felt a strong need to stay put and continue to work full time, learning to know themselves. The girls that chose to remain felt that they had a mission that was different and did not draw them to being adopted out, for now.

***

Now that space for new children was available, Mike's team could start their next plan. This was a tricky bit of business because it required entering a country that had closed borders. It was also a country where females were extremely restricted in their freedom.

Merle was eager to get moving on this assignment. No one was going to restrict her freedom!

Tarita, on the other hand, just enjoyed being a butterfly, so she no longer knew any concept of being restricted.

Mike had his work cut out, trying to keep Merle calm as they proceeded to find the children. They needed to look around without causing attention; even before they got to the border.

The men had been given new identities that showed them as consultants for an international health organization. There were concerns in the region about a virus that was spreading, affecting the muscles in young children. The concern was that if they did not deal it with in time, many children would become paralyzed.

***

They arrived a few weeks early; landing in a neighboring country. They had arranged to work with a university group that acted as consultants for the organization.

The management of this group knew the real reason the men had come and sympathized with their cause. They could not grasp how they intended to get into the country, as they had tried many times over the years without success. They even had to communicate with their citizens via the internet as live meetings could not occur.

Mike just smiled when they voiced their concerns. They did not need to know anything more.

***

About one week into their visit, some members of the university group started receiving messages from their counterparts in the other country that the visibility of the virus had exploded.

At first, the locals said they would deal with the situation on their own, but within a few more days, they had become overwhelmed and recognized they could not deal with the situation on their own and were now requesting outside help.

Now was the chance to get in!

***

The leaders of the little country sent trucks to carry the group, along with some medical supplies. They would not take any chances that people, or any undesirable materials, were going to be spirited in.

These officials spent several precious days investigating the members who would gain permission to enter their domain. When they received the go-ahead, they were loaded into the vehicles for the brief journey.

Several hours later, Mike's team was now in target range. At the assigned hotel, Mike and Tomas sat in their room, preparing for their mission. Using Merle's ability to home in on the target, they determined the children were not far away. What they also needed to know was how they were being contained.

Tarita appeared suddenly, offering to project her butterfly to the location to have a good look.

A few minutes later, she reported back. They were holding the children in a school. Everyone was doing well, but they could not understand what was happening. All they wanted was to go home, even if they did not know where or what that was anymore.

It was becoming a serious situation, so they reached out to Rachel for help.

Soon after they closed their eyes, she appeared. She was listening in, so she knew what to do.

With a flash of her hands over the children, they all writhed in pain, suffering from an extreme case of the virus. Rachel did not like doing this, but it was a necessary step to freeing them.

The officials at the site reported the situation at once. Vehicles arrived at the hotel soon after to whisk the team to the site. Only Mike and Tomas were available to help, as the others were already engaged in other situations.

Upon their arrival at the school, Merle appeared. She turned to the adults in the room and projected sleepy energy at them. They all fell to the floor, comatose.

Rachel then appeared and removed the paralyzing energy from the children so they could load them into a large truck. They were feeling pretty sore from the effects of the virus, however, the chance to go somewhere else was enough incentive to get them moving. Not long after, fifty more children were on their way to the Matrix. Anywhere was better than here!

Getting them out of the country required a bit more work. The children kept quiet as they sat in the back with Tomas. Tarita wanted so much to entertain them as they headed toward their new lives, but she realized this was not the time or place.

They also needed to ensure that the other university members had no difficulties getting back home.

Once on the other side of the border, Mike parked the truck in a forested area. He chuckled as he looked back at the border, where the guards lay slumbering on the ground.

As the adults in the school, they would not even remember what had happened when they woke up.

Rachel appeared again. She waved her hand to end the spell. As fast as the virus had captured the country, it now disappeared. All the children returned to normal.

The next day, the officials held a very expensive dinner for the group (not noticing two missing). They thanked them for their extraordinary work, then drove them back.

As a gift to the country, Merle took charge. Within weeks, the government crumbled when the citizens realized they were prisoners in their own country. This was to be no more. Every person became empowered. They formed a new group to run the country, a place where all people had personal freedom! They could now share with the world!

Chapter 15

There is no such thing as a perfect plan.

Even though Mike's team had rescued the children, they had made a significant mistake.

As Mike and Tomas sat in the briefing room at the university, the project leader informed them, "It seems that there was some misinformation about how the children happened to be in that country."

The men looked at each other astonished.

"The government leaders were paid a very handsome sum to hold the children. The children were not locals, they were kidnapped from a region south of here that has seen nothing but war for years. This complicates things as we now have to start over trying to find out who these people are, and if their parents want them back or if they are even alive."

The men looked at each other again, and in unison said, "I wonder if it is part of the same organization as the first children were rescued from? They will not be very happy with us messing with their merchandise twice."

The project leader continued, "The government agency in charge of such investigations will have their hands full for months now, so don't be expecting to head off home with your new children any time soon. These people thought they were just babysitting them for a while."

***

"What is that you are trying to tell me? The gang leader asked. "What do you mean, the children are gone? I gave them to you to look after until we were ready for them. Do you realize what this means?"

He slammed the phone down. "This is twice now that someone has stolen my merchandise, I am not going to have a business left if this keeps up. It is time for a little secret investigating. I need to find out who is messing with my work."

He was a very secretive man. No one except his closest allies knew his identity. Using this protection, he infiltrated his own gang. He was going to find the weasels that had broken rank.

He thought that the best place to start would be the ones that had lost the first group. He had not heard from them since the situation had occurred earlier in the year.

Since they had not needed to capture any other children except the ones held in the little country, he was not overly suspicious. However, that he had not heard from them at all helped him to decide to go right to their camp.

Arriving with a couple of his henchmen, he was astounded to find the camp completely deserted. There were no signs that there had been any violence. It just looked like they woke up one day and left. It just made no sense.

He spent a couple of days rooting around in the area to see if he could find out anything. Not having any of his local members available, he had no contacts inside the police. Since there was no evidence of violence, he assumed there would have been no police involvement, anyway.

He and his associates visited several sites where they could be holed up, but not a trace. The restaurant where he knew they used as headquarters was even boarded up.

Finally, they heard there was a motorcycle gang not too far away that knew everything that went on, so off they went in search of them. They had been told that they hung out at a bar in a nearby city, so they should not be hard to find. Now if they will just talk!

Later that day, after searching several bars in the city, they finally found the one they were looking for. It was deserted!

There was a padlock on the door and a big For Lease sign hanging in front.

"What the heck is going on?" he raged. "I want to know what is going on. Where are these men? This is too much!"

He banged his fist on the car roof, denting it, but he didn't care. He would flip the car over and burn it right now if he could!

So, what to do now was his most pressing issue. He looked up and down the street. He saw a small grocery store.

"They must have an idea what happened," he said, pointing at the small building.

He entered the store, where an old woman sat behind the counter. He looked at her, giving her his best smile. The old woman cringed, expecting the worst.

"Hello, my dear," he croaked at her. "What has happened to the bar down the street? I was told that a biker gang spent a lot of time there."

She tried to suppress a gleeful grin but just coughed instead.

"The bar went out of business. When the bikers went away, the owner closed it and left town," she said.

"Why did the bikers go away? They usually stay when they find a nice place to hang out."

"Don't know. Maybe you should check the state prison. That is where I would look for them," again trying not to laugh.

The man thought she was being smart; he did not realize she was giving him a clue. Then he thought threatening her might help. As he reached to grab her, the German Shepherd dog laying at her feet jumped up and grabbed his arm.

He immediately pulled his bleeding arm back, painfully realizing his mistake.

"Let's get out of here. I just do not know what to do around this place. It's all crazy around here!" he yelled as he stomped out.

***

The only thing left for him to do was to search the local papers for some potential clues. That was a job for a local as he only spoke minimal English, but did not read it at all.

This would prove very difficult as well.

Heading back toward the city near the airport, one associate tried to find something out by searching the internet, but all he could find was some story back a few years ago about a former cop who had a special skill in solving cold cases.

The man brushed it off, concluding the cop just had dumb luck. At that, he told the driver to take them to the airport.

Nothing had changed. He was going to find out what happened to all these people, but for now, he just wanted to go home and bury his head!

Chapter 16

The principal of a local private school sat at his desk fretting over the school budget, wringing his hands like they were a drenched towel. His school was not affiliated with any church or other organization so, it was struggling. The public school board did not like competition with its schools, so it made fundraising for independents difficult. Money always seemed to be scarce.

***

The children of the Matrix were ready to begin their new lives now that they were all nicely settled in. Local families had now adopted sixteen of the group. Now all the children needed to be enrolled in school. There was concern about having them admitted to public schools since they had not gone to school at all during their whole lives, so they were all going to be much older than the other children in their classes.

The children also wanted to stay together. Rose and her team pondered the problem. There must be a simple way to solve this. They all did research on the internet about local schools. Mike thought he would wander down to the library to see what he could find there.

After reading the local papers, as he was returning them, he began chatting with the librarian.

"You seem to be doing some pretty serious investigating, my friend. Would there be anything I could help you with?" she asked.

"We are looking for a school, likely a private school that might have room for an additional two dozen kids all to start in the same grade asap."

"Am I glad I asked. I know the perfect place for you. And this might just be an answer to a prayer for them as well. With your addition, they might be able to stay open. They have already laid off two teachers because of a tiff with the school board. Seems they do not like private schools. This would at least get one teacher her job back, and all the children could be in the same classroom."

When he returned to the Matrix, Mike gushed out the splendid news. It was a win-win situation that was happening at just the right time.

As soon as she heard the good news. Rose contacted the principal.

"Hello Mr. Peters, this is Rose from the Matrix. I understand that you might have space for an additional classroom of children at your school. They would all be starting in Grade one as they are all foreign language students that do not have a very good grasp of English yet."

The wheels were already in motion, as the principal listened, after picking up the phone from dropping it in excitement. He said. "If you can raise the required funds to rehire one teacher within a week, we could get these children started on their education and save my school.

I have a teacher in mind who is a foreign student specialist. She had many years of experience helping children like the ones from the Matrix. This opportunity is perfect for everyone."

Rose felt strongly about moving forward with the plan, so she called everyone together and led them into a meditation to confer with Rachel.

With a reassuring smile, she said, "*The Cosmic always provides when the conditions are right. A benefactor has been arranged. The money is already on its way to the Matrix bank account as we speak.*

All of these children; even the ones who live with families and are Homo Sapiens are destined to play important roles in the near future of humanity. We must re-educate this teacher into the philosophy of the Matrix, so the children can learn what they need correctly. This is an exciting move forward. It gives me great pleasure to know they will all be together, so they can support each other."

The next day Rose and Beth went to their bank, and sure enough; the money was waiting in the account for them. All of the children would begin learning at the private school the following week.

The next step would be to meet with the teacher and introduce this person to the Matrix. They needed to complement the work they were already doing.

***

The principal contacted the teacher right away and forwarded her name to Rose. They set the meeting up for that afternoon.

She arrived early. It was easy to see that she was very nervous. They welcomed her into the Matrix, but she just did not seem to know how to relax.

Rose was leading the meeting, so she asked her what she could do to help her relax.

"I am a Christian," she replied. "I cannot accept that the work you are doing is the work of my God. Doing yoga and meditating and all the stuff slams the door in the face of all I have ever known."

Rose smiled and suggested they go for a walk around the premises so she could see what they did. She also wanted to tell her about the plight of the children and how well they were doing in this program.

After meeting the children and touring the building, Rose led her outside. She suggested they have a bit of tea and enjoy the fresh air. The woman lived a challenging life. She was exhausted because her heart fought with her mind about how limiting her life was. She could not relax.

Beth brought tea and served it to both ladies. Rose suggested she should take some deep breaths of the fresh air as they sat, as it would help her relax.

The woman passed into a trance as soon as she had drunk the tea, allowing Rachel to appear to her.

"*I am Rachel. I serve the Universal God that created this earth and all that exists. I invite you to join me in this moment of knowing yourself through the eyes of God.*"

With that, she fell deeper into her meditation and soon found herself sitting with her future self, looking back at her future life. She then realized how she could serve her God the very best way by accepting the work of the Matrix as the work of God and as her highest purpose.

After a few moments, she opened her eyes and smiled. "I feel so wonderful now. Thank you. I never realized how having a nice cup of tea outside could help me see so clearly. I do want to work with you.

You know I have to admit that I feel my life has been so limited because I live with beliefs I allow to stop me from coming to terms with my own life. I am looking forward to trying something new."

Everyone looked at her and smiled. Destiny Tea had done its work again. The local laws required all children to attend school, in fact, public school. This principal had found loopholes in the School Act that allowed the private school to operate; however, there were forces in the local establishment that were determined to close it down.

Having the new students and the fresh allotment of cash saved the day for the school. It was a real blessing for the children of the Matrix as well. Rachel had instructed the team that to facilitate growth in the best way possible, the children needed to be exposed to other children so they could experience more than their privileged and secluded life.

The children were all in the same class all the time together, but at recess and lunch, they became part of the student body. Most of the other children just sat and stared at them, especially when they were signing. They had never been exposed to the language of the fingers.

Although bullying was not tolerated, some older children tried to introduce them to the hierarchy. It took very little time for these students to understand that this hierarchy was a thing of the past.

After all, even without invoking their intuitive skills, positive thinking and self-confidence go a long way in changing the attitudes of people who claim they run the world, only because they are bigger.

Within a month, the entire town was buzzing from the impact the Matrix children were having on all the younger population, not just at the private school, but all the children in the town.

These children appreciated being adopted. They did what they were asked because they respected their new parents and understood the value of the bigger picture. They got along with their new siblings and even taught them to be respectful.

Once they could play outside when the weather had warmed up enough, they learned to play games like baseball and soccer, where every one of them excelled.

Maybe a local school would finally win a regional trophy this year! That would be a first!

As they moved up the hierarchy of the town, other children learned to respect them. Even the local bullies became more respectful. Juvenile crime was on the downside, and might even soon disappear.

Acceptance of the new ways still had its minor glitches. Some people on the board were causing trouble, as they did not like the feeling like they were losing control. This was their empire, so they saw this new influence as an invasion of their kingdom.

Something needed to be done about it! The Board of Education was holding its end of the year meeting. It was time to wrap up this year and set the agenda for the new year in the fall.

No matter what else was on the agenda, the powerbrokers on the council were only interested in talking about... and doing something about... the new kids from the Matrix.

It was a closed meeting, so it became more like a war council. However, not everyone was on board with the plan. Not only did they intend to close and destroy the private school but also send the Matrix packing. They did not need this influence in their territory.

How to do this without breaking the law?

That was easy. Change the laws that allowed the private school to exist. They could deal with the Matrix later.

The leader of the group had already studied the rules. She had spoken to a lawyer who supported their agenda and provided her with some proposed changes. As she handed out copies, several members of the council who supported the Matrix children stood in outrage.

They knew this would cause them to be evicted from the meeting. Sliding the papers into their pockets, they prepared to be told to leave.

The ousted members had become familiar with the power of the Matrix group, so when they left the meeting, it did not surprise them to see the team standing outside with the principal and their own lawyer.

The lawyer scanned the handout to ensure he understood its contents and then marched into the meeting room. He walked right up to the president of the council and provided her with his own piece of paper... a Cease and Desist Order.

She was outraged! Nobody was going to stop her, not even with this flimsy document!

She attempted to oust the lawyer and continue with her meeting. These changes needed to be passed this night.

As the lawyer left the room, she giggled out loud... at least until he opened the outside door to allow several police officers in. The next day at the team meeting, Rachel spoke to the group.

"Sometimes it is necessary for us to allow the course of events to unfold at earth level. These lessons need to come to the surface. We already understand the emotional motivation of the council president's agenda. It is important for her true growth that she recognizes herself in this current state before she can be offered the opportunity to reframe.

Remember to stay in the light yourselves, so you can ensure we hold our position and grow stronger when things get tough."

***

The children were all very concerned about what was happening. They knew the woman who was causing all the trouble. They were going to do something to help.

The children talked amongst themselves while they attended classes. They had seen the principal; he looked very upset, so they gathered in the gym after school so they could make a plan.

They had entered through the outside door and left the door open for stragglers. Just as they were about to convene, they heard a noise outside. Suddenly, the room was full to overflowing with children.

Somehow the message had gotten to all the children in town. They all wanted to help. Even though it was not about their school, they knew right from wrong, and they had determined that she was wrong... very wrong.

One of the Matrix children, a girl who had opted to join her new family, took the floor and suggested that she could lead them in a visualization process that would project positive energy to the city and in particular to this woman.

The other children did not know about such a thing, but they knew the Matrix children had special gifts. They all agreed that this was an opportunity to learn something new.

It was difficult for everyone to sit down on the floor, so the bigger kids leaned against the walls, determined to take part.

Soon, the girl began leading the process.

"Follow your breath from your tummy up into your lungs and out of your mouth. Every breath allows you to relax, so your mind can become still."

"Now feel the energy of the earth rise through your feet, rise up your legs, and into your body. At the same time, open the top of your head, so the sky energy can pour down to meet the earth energy at your heart."

She took a deep breath, then continued. "Let the two energies merge and expand until you see yourself in an immense cloud of gold energy. As you continue to breathe deep breaths, help the cloud become denser and larger."

Another deep breath, as she paused again. "See the cloud expand over our entire city. Let the gold energy permeate every individual in our town, including the School Board Council. Keep deep breathing, helping the cloud become stronger and bigger."

One more breath and she exclaimed, "Release the image, and open your eyes."

The loudness of her voice surprised the children, opening their eyes at the sound. They all looked radiant!

Remaining still for a moment. Then pandemonium broke. They were all so shocked by the feelings they had felt during the process. They felt energized, so, within a minute, they had all poured out into the school playground.

As they gathered to chat outside, they realized something different from when they went into the gym. They looked to the street. Their mouths hung open.

Two very busy streets bordered the school. All the traffic... and the people on the sidewalk had come to a complete stop... Nobody stirred for several minutes.

Back at the Matrix, they could all feel what had happened. When they felt the process conclude, they each took a deep breath, opened their eyes, and laughed.

"This ought to be interesting," Mike smiled. "I think we might have a chance." Later in the day, the police and ambulance attended the home of the lady who had chaired the School Board meetings.

When they entered her home, they found her lying unconscious. They found some papers on the table she had been working on that showed the reasons she was so adamant about maintaining control over the schools.

Once the lawyer had filed the papers with the courts, they disbanded the lawsuits. The other members of the board all resigned with a sigh of relief. They had all had enough of political life.

They soon found out; she had gone out of her way to create situations for each of the board members that would cause them extreme embarrassment. It relieved these former council members when the courts ordered this information to be sealed.

Earlier in the day, the woman had been sitting at her kitchen table, going over the documents she needed to keep her position over all the others. As she worked, she chatted with herself, telling her that no power existed that could stop her now.

As she laughed, she gulped, staring at the image that stood in plain view in front of her.

"*I am Rachel. I serve the Universal God that created this earth and all that exists. I invite you to join me in this moment of knowing yourself through the eyes of God.*"

The woman stared at the image speaking at her. She started to wretch, causing her to fall to the floor. She laid there for a moment on her side, then rolled over so she could look Rachel straight in the eyes.

"I do not care who you claim to be. Nothing can stop me from doing what I am doing. I control the people around here and I always will." Then she stopped to take a breath as she went unconscious.

***

Staff at the regional department of education had known of the situation but were not concerned enough to intervene. However, once knowledge of this situation had come to light, the chance to set things straight was upon them.

***

An investigation ensued. They soon discovered she had also blackmailed two regional coordinators. They had set up a way to funnel money from the regional bank accounts into a private bank account she held, to keep her quiet.

***

Upon completion of the investigation, the citizens elected a new council. It was primarily composed of parents who had adopted Matrix children. The heavy cloud that had stifled their lives had now vaporized into the ethers.

Chapter 17

It had been a long, arduous process, but the second group of children was arriving today.

It had been over six months since they had rescued them. One half year of fighting with foreign bureaucracies. Rachel had forewarned them that this process would go like this.

It had to be done on the ground. After all, Rachel could have just waved her hand so their healing could begin as soon as they were out of their prison. However, the governments and other agencies that dealt with orphaned children had to have their input or it would cause more problems down the road.

Mike and Tomas had traveled to the city to visit the children as often as time would allow. Sometimes, even though they represented the host orphanage, the bureaucrats stood their ground and prevented them from having access.

The children had been well taken care of in their new home, although; they were still hostages, but at least they were not prisoners in that strange country anymore. What they needed to comfort them was not available to them, and would not be until they were safely nestled at the Matrix. A big hug would have made such a difference.

Mike and Tomas had a secret method for checking in on the children when the bureaucrats were intent on keeping them out. There were many women hired to look after their needs, but the camp administrators did not seem to keep very good records of who these women were. It was a good thing that people run bureaucracies, often lazy ones!

This made checking in on the children very easy. Merle and Tarita watched the ladies going through the gate a couple of times, noticing what they were wearing and what they did as they entered, then simply copied them.

They were in a non-English speaking country as well, but was not an issue for these special girls either! What language would you like to speak? No hey problemo!

They would take whatever job assigned while inside the camp, but made sure they got to have a good look at the children and interact with them as much as time allowed.

Several times, Tarita displayed her other major talent as well. From her hotel room, she would visualize her golden butterfly, then flutter into the compound as the children slept. As she dusted them with gold dust, she checked their minds to ensure they were feeling safe and cared for. She loved this part of her job!

***

One of the biggest hurdles the community had to face was other children's support agencies. None of them were familiar with the Matrix, so they tried to have them disqualified.

The deciding body, however, was very familiar with the Matrix. They knew how they had rescued the first group last year, and it astounded them, by how they had pulled off the recent rescue.

Nobody ever figured out what caused the virus, why it only affected children, or... how it ended. It was here, then it was gone. Even science can't explain some things!

It was a little touchy at first, but with some metaphysical help, in the form of gold light, the board concluded the Matrix held the best option for the children. Not seeking financial support from anyone was the final straw that saw the children heading for their new home, with Mike and Tomas leading them.

***

The children fidgeted about as they stood in line, waiting for their new and unknown future. It was understandable they were feeling in a quandary about being shipped off to some place, not only had they never been to before, but had never even heard of either. It was scary enough being in the camp; however, being held hostage for far too long in the neighboring country and having had to live through that terrible virus, they let themselves find solace in being able to start a new life, even though they had no idea what they were in for.

They found solace in the ladies. Already knowing Merle and Tarita from their secret visits as working ladies, the children accepted they were going to a better place. They found peace when they heard they would get to go to school and live with other children, and get to do kid things.

As soon as they were in the hands of the Matrix group, Mike and Tomas were the representatives they met first. This was a little unsettling because they were expecting Merle and Tarita. However, Tomas explained the ladies were at their office preparing for the journey to their new home. He promised them they would see them later that day.

And sure enough, the ladies made their appearance that afternoon. When they saw them, they started jumping and dancing in excitement. For the first time, they felt good with people they knew, liked, and were starting to trust.

Merle and Tarita spent several hours with the children singing songs (of course in their language!), dancing, being silly, and just playing around. The little people had never known such a fun time! They daydreamed about having this much fun every day in their new lives. They could hardly contain themselves.

As a special treat, Tarita told them stories about butterflies while the children danced and fluttered like the butterflies they were hearing about.

Too soon, it was sleepy time, so they could be prepared for tomorrow's big adventure. Merle told the children that she and Tarita were going on ahead this night, so they could have everything ready for them when they arrived at the Matrix. Some children wanted to object, but Merle just smiled and told them they would be together there for many years, so there was plenty more time to be together.

***

Not much sleep this night for these little munchkins, feeling way too excited for such a trivial thing as sleep! They all had packed what little they owned into packsacks Tomas had purchased for them so they would be ready after the crack of dawn.

Breakfast done, everyone loaded onto the bus, heading to the airport. The government agency that had awarded the Matrix custody of the children had done a superb job of providing the documents for their exit. Some of the officials even came to see them off. They were pleased, and surprised, how happy and well-behaved the children were. It seemed like they were going on a vacation.

The flight and following bus ride were long. Most of the children slept during the flight, so they were wide awake once they were back on the ground. None of them had any idea what waited ahead for them, but knowing that Merle and Tarita were going to be there, good things seemed inevitable.

As the buses unloaded, Rose, Beth, Teesha, and Sheila came out to greet them. Mike and Tomas slipped away while the ladies distracted the children. After they had made all the greetings, Beth asked them who they wanted to see, and with a resounding echo they all screamed, "Merle and Tarita"!

They made such a grand entry for the children, donning funny hats and blowing whistles as they ran out to greet them. It was hard to tell that these people had suffered so much terror in their little past. They were just like regular kids.

With all the basic stuff sorted out, they invited the children down to the yoga room. There, the staff introduced them to all the children they had rescued in the first run. This was the first time as well that the adopted children had joined in for a celebration at the Matrix. Everyone, including the new ones, were beside themselves with excitement.

For about one minute, they were a little shy, but it didn't take long to get over that bit of business, as the kids all ran outside to see the gardens and the forest. These are always guaranteed hits for kids! The older kids also knew what it felt like to be new in a strange home.

It was a little hard for them to speak verbally together, but the older children started right away teaching them to sign. Soon, they were all laughing and playing together, speaking with their hands.

Chapter 18

Mike and Tomas had been away from the Matrix for a long while, preparing for the new flock of children to be transported to their new home. Once they were back, they craved to get started on a very significant project that would require very careful planning and treatment... for a very long time.

The boys from the original group that had claimed they felt something kicking inside them needed to be prepared for their future... a distant future, but still their future. There was no denying what the kicking was about.

At least they would get to prepare for the event, unlike Mike and Tomas, who were thrown into it unprepared in any way. They were determined these youngsters would be ready when the time came.

Meeting with Rachel was the first thing that needed to happen. The next afternoon, they relaxed in the team conference room, settling into a meditation.

Rachel studied the three of them for a moment, then said:

"It is good that we begin preparing these boys for their future, a future that will not be denied, so let us begin. Each of these people is Homo integratis. They have about two years before they will transition into their full being. It will be onset as their bodies prepare to enter puberty. As the hormones of the oncoming adulthood increase for them as males, the hormones of female will also increase.

They must learn now that the changes they will embrace as Homo integratis are natural, and by Cosmic design. You must help them not only to integrate these changes and make peace with themselves through their integration. We must also prepare them for the special talents they will learn to express. Michael and Thomas, since you know better than any other the importance of this project, you will co-lead through your own inspiration. The future needs these individuals to be prepared well."

Rachel then smiled at the three of them, slowly fading into the ethers; but as a final word, she said, "There are others; watch for them."

***

Before the men could help the boys work through their stuff, they needed to consecrate the unfolding of their own journey. It would require a clear mind, clearer communication, and an unconditional relationship with Merle and Tarita.

Even though both of the men could feel and sense their female counterparts when they became active; they basically went to sleep. It was now imperative that all four of them learn to work with each other's counterpart in a wide-awake state.

Until now, when Merle or Tarita appeared, usually either the other's male counterpart was absent or they both transitioned at the same time, so Merle and Tarita and Mike and Tomas had not really been exposed to the other's opposite. They were only familiar with the same gender aspect of the other. This needed to change.

For them to be fully engaged, they needed to be completely familiar with both aspects of the other person, including working with whoever expressed in that situation.

To start the process, Mike and Tomas decided they should begin this new learning curve away from the Matrix so they could reduce the stress of worrying about being interrupted, especially by the boys.

Sheila had a friend who owned a cabin at a remote lake not far away. She suggested they might enjoy a vacation to recover from their very busy year. How about some fishing? What a great cover!

***

With a car filled with groceries and fishing gear, they arrived at their destination. It was perfect. They found the cabin at the end of a dirt road where there were no other cabins nearby, and right beside a beautiful little lake.

Once settled in, they found a pleasant spot on a little knoll just above the edge of the lake. Sitting a bit apart from each other, they closed their eyes. Taking slow, deep breaths, relaxing, moving out of the way, so Merle and Tarita could express.

The change happened quickly. They both opened their eyes and sat peering out at the wonderful view. Even a fish jumped out of the water for them!

They sat for a long time, embracing the feelings of being in the forest by the lake. Such a wonderful grounding but uplifting feeling!

Tarita could not resist. She had to let out her inner butterfly so it could enjoy being in its most natural place. The intense excitement of this moment was almost too much for her, but she knew there was serious work that needed to start right away.

They looked at each other and intuitively decided they should switch one at a time, so Merle closed her eyes and relaxed, allowing Mike to return. When he opened his eyes, he saw Tarita staring wide-eyed at him. She smiled, then ran over and gave him a big hug.

They both agreed that it was quite amazing watching the transition happen, as they chatted away about nothing, just getting used to each other. They had not known what happened during the change before, since they went dormant while it occurred.

They both closed their eyes and relaxed again, allowing both of their other halves to show. Tomas and Merle sat studying each other. They both laughed and hugged. This was such a relief for all of them. They were now real to each other.

They were fortunate that both individuals; no matter which personality, were mature enough to manage their egos. Getting to know each other could become a problem if any of them decided they wanted to express themselves whenever they chose, to the detriment of the other aspect, or the situation they were working in.

This left them with a dilemma, though. Who would get to be expressed when?

There were no external factors to help determine when who was to be outside and who would be inside. After all, they could not both be in the physical at the same time... yet.

The critical lesson needing to be integrated right now was an internal process for both of them; how to communicate with their own other aspect instead of going to sleep. To support this, they decided that since the male aspect was the home base, they would be male unless the female aspect could better complete a task. (No sexism here!)

Mike and Tomas then focused on preparing the cabin for their stay, followed by a scrumptious meal to be enjoyed by all.

***

With everything in place for optimal creature comfort, Mike and Tomas turned to the lesson at hand... learning how to communicate with their other.

They both found a nice spot by the lake, but this time, they sat far apart so they would not interfere with each other's concentration. Closing their eyes, they concentrated on their breaths.

Once they had attained the required amount of attunement, they called the name of their counterpart. It took quite a while to make any headway. Now that they knew what the other looked like in the physical; it was easier to visualize them. This helped, but it still required more.

They could feel they were being supported, but they were not sure where the help was coming from. Rachel then appeared.

"*Focus on feeling your counterpart. What does feminine energy feel like to you? Let your male energy subside to allow your consciousness to accept the female. Michael, do you remember when Merle came to you during the Kundalini lessons? Try to go there."*

Soon, they each could feel their female aspect. It was a beautiful feeling, so robust and warm. The energy continued to increase, feeling like a blender that was slowly churning to create a new blended energy that was both male and female at the same time.

It was now like they were in the same room; only it was actually they were in the same body. They began communicating by looking at each other as if they were in a dream, only they were awake. Each one could move themselves freely as if they were each in their own body.

Gradually, they began making faces at each other. When this was not entertaining enough, they got on their feet, jumping and dancing on their own at first, then together like they had choreographed a dance scene from a broadway movie.

They laughed and laughed, realizing they liked each other. They were comfortable with their unusual situation.

Rachel then reappeared, instructing the men to open their eyes. Both of the girls screamed in delight, as they could see the world through their male eyes. They could hardly resist jumping out of themselves.

Rachel told the men to relax their bodies and allow the women to move their body parts as they chose. The ladies explored with their fingers, feeling all the parts, moving them just to make it more real. For a long time, the girls prodded and touched all over the men's bodies, becoming familiar with them.

As they became more confident, they caused the men to stand up and walk around the area. They stopped along the way to take in the plants, trees, squirrels, and the fantastic view of the lake. What an amazing experience.

Switching around was much easier since they now had physically communicated, but Tomas quickly got thrown for a loop when Tarita abruptly released her inner butterfly.

She transformed so fast, she almost caused an accident. Tomas was completely unprepared for the transition. Being a fast thinker, though, Tarita swooped her wings down cocooning him, then pulling him back inside so she could regain her balance and Tomas could share her beautiful sense of freedom.

At sunset, Mike was sitting on a knoll, enjoying the view. He could feel Merle was close, so he closed his eyes. She came to him. She wanted to talk about something that she had held back for a long time. It was the start of his magical power.

"When you prayed to the Universe that day back when you were still small, you gave birth to me. Before that moment, I was just an aspect of you, that may have never been realized. When you prayed, you gave me permission to become... and I did. But I did not know how to let you know about me, so I just worked inside of you.

I was very young and innocent to the world at that time too, so I did not mind staying on the inside, however, I was getting anxious to play out in the world too. I guess I was feeling cooped up. I did not like the way your life was going and I wanted to do something about it.

When your father came at you, bent on your destruction, I knew it was time to act. I instinctively reacted to protect you by projecting that force field out of your hands that caused your father to have that meltdown. That was the dawn of my life within you, and the beginning of the possibilities that are now developing for both of us.

As you learned how to master the power, you refined it so you could use it how you liked. I enjoyed being a part of your life during this time, however, as you grew more comfortable, I felt a growing need to express myself distinctly from you. The only way I knew to reach out to you was to cause you those headaches."

***

Part two began the following morning. The aim was to have each person work with; as well as independently, from their other aspect.

Today's activity was game playing!

In the cabin were many board games, so each person was to pick a game, setting it up for the two aspects to work as opponents. This would have great value because it would show, first, that they can think separately from each other. Second, it would let each of them watch and analyze how the other person thinks, and third, hopefully, it would show how they relate to each other when working individually.

Mike and Merle chose Monopoly while Tomas and Tarita chose Scrabble. They set the games up and dove in.

Mike and Merle were each very competitive, so they quickly began developing as big a property profile as they could. Each time they made a big move, they would laugh and whack the other one lovingly.

Tomas and Tarita were not so competitive but were master Scrabble players. They strategically set up the board creating some genius moves, however, they deliberately created a wide-open board so there were lots of openings. Each time they played a turn, they laughed and congratulated each other. A tight game ensued with scores heading into championship level.

Back at the Monopoly board, Merle was trying hard to win over Mike, but he was no slacker and was not giving in easily. Merle eventually pulled away when Mike kept landing on her properties. She had masterminded a strong trap for him by buying several properties close together, then loaded them with houses. One stop at Chez Merle was very costly for Mike!

Scrabble is a much shorter game than Monopoly, so by the time Mike and Merle had completed their one game, Tomas and Tarita were in the middle of the third of their games; the tiebreaker. They each had less than seven tiles left. The score was close. Which one would be the champ?

The score was now tied with each only having two one-pointers left. They sat quietly for a moment, then turned their tiles over, abdicating the game. The room became very full of love at that moment.

In the meantime, Mike had fought a tough battle. Merle was a good competitive player. Losing or giving in was not in her vocabulary!

There would be other opportunities Mike!

**

After a well-earned break consisting of walking in the woods while sipping hot tea and chomping down cookies, they returned to the house and jumped into the next game: Trivial Pursuit. This time it was to be four individuals!

All four were pretty smart cookies and excellent strategists, so this was going to be an exciting game. Alex Trebek would have been proud to be the host!

The challenge in this game would be for each of them to support, and allow their other aspect to appear and retreat quickly, fully, and often. With such intelligent players, the game could move fast, however, it took a bit for the transitions to occur easily enough to keep the game flowing naturally.

It became difficult to keep up with whose turn it was. The rotations became quick and complete. For this to happen; they each had to learn how to help the other appear, then wait, then withdraw. By the end of the game, they were pros.

The final event was a card game where they played teams. As a twist though, it was boys against girls. This was tough! Each player would have to figure out how to play without exposing their hand to their other aspect. This meant learning how to shield information, a powerful skill to have for the work coming up!

The girls won, of course, because they had an advantage... telepathy! It's more of a girl thing, so the boys really did not have a chance.

Soon the day was about to wrap up. They were glad they had a couple more days to spend in the forest... all this heavy work exhausted them. As they relaxed, they all could hear Merle snickering.

To Mike's embarrassment, she let it out that they had made a side bet on the Monopoly game. Since Merle won, she got to choose what they would wear for the next week!

Chapter 19

Back at the Matrix, the ladies got together to work with the boys. They wanted them to be initiated into their new training program by the time Mike and Tomas returned. These boys had a lot to learn about themselves and their future over the next short while, so anything that would ease them into it a little easier would be helpful.

Teesha was first out of the gate. She knew some special yoga moves that would help them balance the Yin & Yang or male and female sides of their being. This was also an easy and stress-free way to start the boys off on their journey to their new wholeness since they already enjoyed playing yoga.

These fellows were going to have a much easier time learning about themselves now that they had been part of the Matrix household for over a year. They had seen a lot of things that children in the outside world would never see in a lifetime, so things that might be weird to others would be more commonplace to them.

Another advantage for them as well was all the clearing that they had done. Had this not happened, these boys would likely be members of a criminal gang, street urchins, or perhaps even be dead. They were supremely fortunate.

Having cleared any of the trauma and dysfunctional beliefs they had learned in their former life, they were all very settled and real as people... something one rarely sees even in children raised in healthy normal families.

They were eager to learn about anything that became available. They were all getting quite good at yoga, meditating, visualizing, and even their schoolwork. If there were ever children ready to take on this new life, these were the most likely.

***

Mike and Tomas had arrived back the evening prior, to prepare for the start of their new program. When they arrived at the yoga room the next morning, the boys were already playing yoga, so they joined in.

The original children that remained at the Matrix stayed as a group, even sharing rooms in the living quarters. They interacted with the second group over the day and even had some sessions with them, but they were separate, sort of like a bunch of older brothers.

The staff preferred they maintain the separation as well so it would be emotionally easier for them as they matured and when some unusual changes began to happen.

They gathered all the remaining original children, so they could discuss what was about to happen. The newest group was not ready, by any means, to learn anything intense yet, as they were still working on assimilating into the Matrix lifestyle. They invested much of their day, focused on clearing the traumas from their lives. After all, how could they turn into the amazing people they were born to be if they were still carrying around a bunch of unnecessary baggage?

After yoga, the boys gathered in a smaller room along with all the training staff. Mike first explained a bit about what they were going to be doing in this group, then he turned the lead over to Sheila to explain the basic concepts.

"This is an exciting adventure you are embarking upon, which will go on for the rest of your life. We will provide you with the training you will need, so you get a satisfactory understanding. You must integrate these concepts into your lives now because any misunderstandings may be harder to correct later. In this, Mike has asked me to speak to you today.

The yoga moves Teesha has been teaching you of late, have been a particular form designed to harmonize your male and female aspects. This is critical as it brings us to the most important basic fact related to what we are striving for.

All human beings carry aspects of both male and female energy. It is one way that the Creator had implemented that keeps us balanced. All of you were born into a male body; however, you each have female traits to ally with your male side. A simple example is your appreciation of nature. How many of you genuinely enjoy going out in the backyard so you can smell the flowers and touch the trees?"

They all raised their hands, so she continued, "Caring is another female trait ... as well as nurturing.

When you help a friend... that is a female trait, because it is nurturing."

"How do you determine which is male and which is female Sheila?" asked one boy.

"Good question! We generally consider female energy passive or not requiring a physical action to carry it out, while male energy is active. It does not matter the gender of the person carrying out the action; we still class the energy as the same. If a girl plays soccer; she uses her male energy to play the game as she focuses to win. To be great at the game she needs to express her inner male. And if a man chooses to be a skilled chef, it is his inner female that carries the passion for the creative side of cooking.

As society evolves, the male of our species is becoming less dominant. The days of the man being the breadwinner by working horrific hours out in the fields or in factories have become diluted as recent inventions have replaced much of the hard work. And now women are finding meaningful jobs in industries that used to be exclusive domains for men. The result is that the male energy has become less vital. To remain healthy, men need to adapt. No place for egos.

Another key factor stimulating this change is the increase in interest in what we call mindful practices: meditating, yoga, personal development, etc. The result is that men are becoming more balanced in their yin & yang. Now they actually help to raise the children and clean the house, where before that was a woman's domain.

Because of all these changes, we, as a species, are changing and evolving to live at a higher spiritual level; so much so that a new species of human has appeared. These people are born in such a way that they can operate in a much more powerful manner with their inner male and female. We are going to talk about this more soon. I just wanted to give you this information so you could think about it."

It impressed Mike how Sheila had handled the talk. He especially liked that she did not divulge all the information at one time. Build up to it... What a great idea!

Mike then suggested they all stand up and do some quick yoga moves to get their blood moving again. This had been quite a stimulating session.

"The next step for today is a meditation. We are going to have Tomas lead it... Tomas," Mike said, turning to his friend.

At first, Tomas was a little nervous. He had never led a session before, but his confidence soared when he felt a little kick from inside. This would be his first time working with Tarita as an integrated person.

Tomas moved to center position, sitting on the power chair. He motioned for everyone to step into meditation position. Following suit, they each focused on their breath, building up their connection with Source.

"Visualize a spot about 18 inches above your head. We call this the Star Chakra. It is the first chakra inside your energy field from Source. See the Cosmic energy in the sky flow down into this gateway, then see the energy continue down into your Crown Chakra at the top of your head. Make sure your Crown Chakra is open, so the energy can move down into and through your body."

"Visualize a spot in the earth about 18 inches below your feet. Pull the energy up with your breath from this center, pulling it through your feet, up your legs, and finally meeting the sky energy in your solar plexus, in the center of your body. Meld the energies together by seeing them blending, as you continue your focused breaths."

"Feel your own consciousness and pull it into the energy in your solar plexus until all becomes one. Continue breathing deeply."

As they all followed his instructions, the energy in the room increased so much. No one had ever experienced such a high before... and they were far from done yet!

"Using normal breaths, while concentrating on this energy, visualize it expanding away from your body. Keep expanding it well beyond your own energy field, letting it combine with the energies of everyone in the room. Let it keep expanding to fill the whole Matrix. Keep breathing and focusing on the energy!"

"See it expand throughout the entire town... the entire country... the entire planet... the entire Universe. Hold your focus. Hold... Hold... Hold.

Now, let yourself loose in your focus, and just be."

Sometime later, Tomas spoke again. "Focus on your breath. Start pulling the energy back to you; draw it back from the connection with Source, bringing it back with you. Draw it back from your focus on our planet. Breathe. Draw it back into this room, and with a final breath, draw it back into your Solar Plexus, and hold it there."

After a few minutes, he concluded, saying "When you are ready; take a deep breath and come back to the room by opening your eyes."

He sat patiently, waiting. After a few minutes, all the adults and four of the boys sat quietly with their eyes open, staring into space. Tomas nodded to Beth and Sheila to intervene with the two remaining boys.

They softly approached, then kneeled on the floor in front of them, placing the tips of their fingers on the toes of the boy in front of them. Deep breathing, then holding their breath, they visualized them being grounded here on earth.

Taking big breaths, then opening their eyes, Beth and Sheila remained in position to make sure they were back; then tiptoed back to their seats.

No one else moved or spoke for a long time. They just sat, enjoying the feeling of connection.

Finally, Tarita could not sit still any longer, so she took Tomas for a victory lap around the room as her golden butterfly. They had truly become one, as he held on tight.

Chapter 20

Beth and Sheila were now working with the new children. They had already collected a long list of applicants who were wanting to adopt a "Child of the Matrix" as they had fondly come to be known.

It was the dream both women shared, to be part of a program that was designed to help traumatized children transform into normal, healthy people. It became obvious by the acceptance of and demand for Children of the Matrix; they had definitely realized their dream.

Local families had adopted the available children, and so far, were doing very well. In fact, the adopting families were doing much better as well.

It never ceased to amaze them that a child with a healthy sense of self-realization could make such a tremendous impact on the people around them... just by being there!

Now that the second group had arrived, the remaining boys were ready to help these children do some amazing work as well. In the first few days these kids had been there, the older ones made sure the new kids were fast on the way to being adept at signing. After all, kids like to chat with each other!

Magda was likely the happiest person in the world as she watched over her flock!

Having the children from the first group here to assist throughout the retraining process was a godsend, but the new children still had some serious work to do on their own. After all, when it comes to one's own personal growth, nobody else can do the work for you. Others can guide you, but the actual work is up to you.

These children had really suffered. There were definite signs of physical and mental abuse. They had all been deprived of good food as well, so helping them develop healthy bodies was early on the list. Reframing any beliefs about being starved and going without would be paramount.

Beth, Sheila, and Teesha let themselves feel sad for the children for a moment, however, they knew that the suffering was part of their Karma; for if their life had been different; they might not be here with them today. They made sure that the children understood that as well. Any playing the victim was quashed immediately.

After all, it is out of adversity that comes the greatest growth!

One particular girl had really suffered. She looked emaciated and walked with a limp.

Rather than letting her stay in victim; they targeted her to be their next hero. This girl would find her wings and fly! What they didn't realize was that this statement was far truer than they thought!

As they led the children through the paces of learning the reframing processes, this girl became really quick at clearing herself. She said she did not like the way she felt, and so she was going to help herself feel better. She became so good at it they had to create some extra barriers to keep her from doing it too quickly.

One day, a few months after they had arrived, Tarita was leading the children in a visualization process. They were learning to connect with the energy of nature. As she led the group through the session, she realized there was another butterfly in the visualization! This little girl was indeed an amazing little soul!

This created a bit of a conundrum for the trainers as she now stood (or "flew" more correctly), alone in her class. She could not train with the boys in the earlier group because their Karma was different, but she was too advanced to maintain her growth in her current group. What to do?

***

When Tarita finished her session, they took a break. This was a perfect opportunity to consult with Rose. Finding her in her office working on some paperwork, Rose smiled, relieved to have a reason to stop. When Beth explained the problem; she suggested they have a conference with Rachel.

Once they were in the right state; Rachel immediately appeared to them, saying, "*I have been watching this child. She is indeed special. You will really need to pay attention to her progress if she is to achieve her best. She has figured out how to move through the reframing process without truly doing the work she needs to clear herself.*

Without completing the process adequately,
she will become a problem, as she still operates on
some dysfunctional beliefs that may cause her to
make poor decisions.

Please remember, the purpose for anyone
connected with the Matrix is to speed up their spiritual
growth. Anyone trying to take shortcuts must be
stopped and corrected immediately.

We must take this girl back to step one of the
clearing process and begin again. If she continues to
resist making the changes and clearing properly, I will
intervene. In the meantime, I have clipped her wings.
If she tries to fly again; she will find her feet still on the
ground. Hopefully, this will create the incentive to get
her doing the work as it needs to be done.

I will be watching closely," she said as she
faded away.

"Looks like we really have our work cut out for
us with this little girl!" Rose commented. "Let's do
some energy work on her, and try to cause her to
shift."

The women then began their relaxation
process so they could do the visualization work. Once

they had achieved the right level of focus, they each saw her in their mind and began directing gold light at the little girl. At first, the girl resisted absorbing the flow of gold light, but soon it became too much for her to block and began letting it in.

They could feel the difference in her mindset as she let go. Soon, she was wide open to accepting the energy.

When they met the little girl later, she was definitely a different person.

Beth took her aside and quietly chatted with her so she could understand more about what had been going on that was creating the resistance.

"When I was still living with my parents, my life was very scary," she started. "Big mean men constantly came into all the homes in our area. They took whatever they wanted when they came. They even took our food. Sometimes they stayed a long time as they forced my mother to cook them an enormous meal. My father was a very big, tough man, but he could do nothing to protect us from this group of men. Even the police were too afraid. The men claimed they were protecting the people, and they needed to have what they wanted to be strong, for the residents to feel safe."

"I learned how to become a butterfly so I could escape. One day when they were leaving my house; they grabbed me and forced me to go with them. My father and mother tried to stop them, but they couldn't."

"That is when I learned to become a butterfly. I often became a butterfly so I could fly back home to see my parents. They were so sad, but they could not see me; no matter how much I fluttered my wings," she sobbed.

Beth responded by giving her a reassuring hug. She then led her into a clearing visualization. It took many more sessions to help her clear the old memories. Eventually, they dissolved away.

They kept the little girl in her original class with her mates. She was happy about that, as it gave her a sense of comfort. It took many months before Rachel let her fly again, but when she finally got her wings to work, she was a completely different person!

Chapter 21

A man with a bad temper is not a man to fool with.

He was going to find out who was responsible for not only one, but two major thefts of his property.

Everything had gone well for years. He had made millions of dollars from expropriating children from their parents. Why did the parents' care? They could just make more! They are nuisance little things, anyway. Better to sell them into slavery and be done with them!

There was very little that made this man smile; except when he had a bunch of brats to dump off on some idiots that were willing to give him money, so they could do whatever they liked with them.

As he sat stewing about this calamity, he was trying to figure out what had happened. He had tried again and again to contact both groups. The first one had completely disappeared as if they had never existed. The other group, well no point in trying to talk to them, as they were likely all in jail since the coup in their country. Imagine; throwing out a perfectly good government, just so the people could have rights!

In a moment of something close to sanity, he had instructed one of his boys to do some more research. All they could come up with was this guy that rode a motorcycle and drew pictures of crime scenes. No one knew any more about him.

He sent one of his people to infiltrate the group that had helped to steal the children from him in the closed country. He had heard it was two women that had pulled off the heist, but the agency told them it was two men that helped with clearing the virus.

Eventually, he became so frustrated, he sent these two unreliable snitches to a place where they could think about their incompetence for a very long time.

***

Mike kept getting this odd feeling that there was something not quite right in his world. It was like someone was mad at him. Believe me; there were few people upset with this boy! He had helped pull off miracles in recent times that made many people thrilled... But the feeling niggled at him.

He consulted with Merle. She knew everything that had gone on... in fact; it was she that had perpetrated much of it. With her keen intuitive senses, she should be able to figure out what he was feeling... and more importantly, what his higher self was trying to communicate with him.

They were so well connected now that there was no special process needed to chat. She did not invade his space much; she was probably off doing her own thing; however, she pulled that off... without a body... since Mike was busy using it.

Anyway, as soon as Mike called to her, Merle appeared to him in his mind. He asked her if she could tap into this feeling to see if she could get to the root of it. With a deep breath, she went silent for a moment, then stared at him, looking absolutely aghast!

"The government of that little country did not kidnap those children, Mike," she reported. "In fact, it was the same gang as the ones who kidnapped the first group we collected. What it appears you are feeling is the anger of the leader of the kidnapping organization. He is venting into the Universe at you. Lucky for us; he cannot figure out who you are."

"Then that is a good thing for me, and even better, you discovered him before he has time to find me. Any suggestions, Merle?"

"Hmmm. I think this requires consultation with Rachel. We have to have the full picture of this. There may be more to this than we might know."

They prepared to contact Rachel. As he began; Mike laughed "This is the first time we have actually had a meeting with Rachel together in consciousness!"

Merle gave him a little kick in fun as they settled in.

"*Discovering this situation without his being aware gives us a considerable advantage. It pleases me to see how well you connect into Universal Consciousness. What you have found is accurate.*

Be still and calm regarding this situation. It needs to play out more yet. Your ability to connect with his consciousness is the tool we need to discover when he has kidnapped any more children. I suggest you connect with him periodically, so you can read his mind. *As soon as he has more children; we will prepare another visit.*"

"Why don't we just stop him now before he hurts any more people?" Mike asked.

"*He does not know that he is doing us a service. He thinks he is a bad person when in reality he is collecting children who are destined to be a part of the Matrix family. It is part of their karma that they need to suffer deeply so they will be able to access the great strength they hold inside themselves. In time, as humanity evolves, there will be an easier method to bring forward the amazing strength held inside so many people, so they can express their life purpose to the fullest. For now, we have to use the tools we have at this consciousness level, making sure we collect these children as quickly as possible, so we can clear them and help them become the amazing individuals they are.*"

As Rachel faded back into Source, she reiterated, "*Make sure you keep checking in on him, Merle.*"

***

Sure enough, it was not long before Merle discerned he was collecting another group of children. He had a customer who was prepared to take all of them. This person had even prepaid for the whole lot. (Obviously, this customer had not been aware of the last botched attempts!)

Merle continued to drop in on his thoughts periodically, trying to get the location where the children were being held. This girl was a first rate gumshoe. She dug and dug, trying to discover any pertinent information that might help or impede their foiling of his entrepreneurship.

"He never learns, does he?" she laughed as he finally coughed up the information.

"The children are being held in a large ship that is tied up at a port right near where we rescued the last group. At least we know our way around the area now. I am trying to get more information about the site. He will likely have a lot of guards on duty. He can't afford to lose another deal, or he will be out of business."

"Do you know who he sold them to?"

Merle picked through the man's mind... a disgusting but necessary task. This man would never be in her top ten!

A few minutes later she spoke "I have it. The man lives in a large house on an island far out in the ocean. It is like a fortress. What are you thinking, Mike?"

"Well, Rachel said that he has not completed his work for us yet, so if we go in and ruin his deal, he is likely going to be furious... and more importantly, he will lose face in his community and not be able to continue helping us. I think we should let him deliver them, and then collect them from his customer."

"How do you suggest that?" Merle laughed, knowing full well what he was thinking. "You really are a devious character, aren't you! I am glad we are sharing the same body!"

***

Before they could embark on their next escapade to collect the children, there were preparations needed, both for the mission, and here at the Matrix.

Consulting with Rose, they agreed they needed to push the newer children forward to prepare them for the receiving of their new brothers and sisters. Since they would now be the middle children, the concern was that their noses could get out of joint.

Beth and Sheila joined in the meeting right away, but it was Teesha who was the problem solver again.

"We need to get the children excited about these new children arriving. It will be just like when Mom and Dad are preparing to bring a new sibling home from the hospital."

Everyone laughed and congratulated her on such a brilliant suggestion. Teesha then offered that she should ramp up the yoga training and get Magda to do the same with the signing.

"While we are doing this; we can chat to them about the new children coming to join them, that have suffered through the same tragedies they went through."

Everyone agreed and set about getting everything set up. There were no concerns about having enough space at the Matrix, considering they had not even opened up the wing that Merle had gifted to them so long ago. Also, several of the girls in the original group had warmed up to the idea of being adopted after they realized what a glorious life the other adopted children were having. This left only the six boys from group one.

**

Merle kept checking in on the gang leader to see how he was progressing with transferring the children. According to what she picked up, they were still on the ship, but he was not ready to move. He wanted them to chill until he was safely back at his home base and out of the way.

In the meantime, the fearless foursome got prepared to head over to a city closer to the buyer's island. They wanted to get there early to do final preparations and to get a feel for the locale, including visiting the local police.

Merle astral traveled there so she could get a better picture of the energy of the location. She could see the city clearly from above, but she needed to get her feet on the ground so she could get a better feeling. She had never done this before, but then she had done lots of things since she was given the chance to express on her own that she had never done before. So, off she went, at first hovering over the city, getting an overview of its location. When she felt confident enough; she willed herself down to the ground and returned to the physical.

She landed in a small, wooded park that was near the downtown core. Taking her time connecting with the trees to help her get grounded, then she checked in to make sure Mike had come with her. He had.

"Good," she said. "We can both do our part here. Since you are a retired cop, you can handle the local gendarmes. I want to get a feel for the buyer's connections in this city. He must have to get supplies to feed his people... even orphans have to eat!"

***

Sometimes it is tricky having two minds in one body, but the one thing that Mike and Merle had learned to do, as a matter of survival, was to cooperate. To complete assessing the feeling of the town, it did not matter who was on the outside, as they now could work together and separately at the same time. They just could not physically be in two places at once... yet.

The police station would be the first stop. This was a small city, so it was easy to find it. Mike had kept his insurance investigator's badge from days long gone; it would come in handy right now. Just by showing it to the cop at the front desk; before long, he was sitting in front of the sergeant in charge.

Mike told the sergeant that they were investigating the man who lived on the island for insurance fraud. He did not tell him they were there to collect the children. Mike asked him about the specifics of the island.

He pulled out a map and explained all the details, including the layout of the island and the buildings. The most important note he revealed was the supply ship that was in the harbor would return to the island the next day.

He did not know who the key suppliers for the island's needs were, but in wrapping up the meeting; Mike learned that if there was any criminal activity he uncovered; he had men available to clean up.

Mike smiled and laughed to himself. This police station better have a big jail!

Mike then walked down to the dock to have a look at the ship that carried the supplies to the island. It was already loading some goods from a cartage truck with the logo of a local store on the side.

Several men, obviously longshoremen, were busy unloading the goods from the truck to the cargo deck on the ship. Mike joined in the unloading. The men smiled when Mike offered to help, as there was a lot of work to get done in a short time. They said if they got done early, they would get extra pay and the boat could sail early.

While they were loading the boat; Merle used her extrasensory skills to scan the layout. Since the island was quite a long way off the shore, there was a cafeteria. If she could find the women's locker room, she should be able to find a uniform and join the kitchen staff.

As the crew finished loading the boat, Mike made sure he was on it. He quietly stole away from the loading area to find a secluded spot where Merle could have her turn.

***

Merle was in her element. Catching the bad guys was her thing! This was the opportunity of a lifetime to catch one bad dude! She did not want to know what this man needed the children for; she just wanted to get them out of there and get them to the Matrix.

Nobody paid attention to the new girl on the job. She could see what needed to be done, so she jumped right in. Speaking their dialect made her cover even more believable.

It took a full twenty-four hours of sailing to complete the trip, so it gave Merle enough opportunity to scope out the ship and the crew. They would need to get the children on the boat once they completed the rescue mission. She laughed as she realized they would also need a large enough room to host the man and his gang as well!

The captain seemed to be a reasonable person and friendly toward his crew. He did not recognize Merle but welcomed her on board. This gave her a great opportunity to size him up, to prepare for the return voyage. She found out the ship would remain tied up at the island's dock for two days until it needed to return for more supplies.

She also learned that the crew had jobs on the island as well. This was perfect!

She had the perfect cover for infiltrating the island without being noticed. Now if she can just get either herself or Mike a job that requires entering any of the buildings on site so they could find out where the children are and their condition.

**

The island was not at all large. They could explore the entire island in a couple of hours. There were several houses and outbuildings large enough to contain the children... if they even had them contained!

Merle remained very busy on the ship right until they were ready to disembark, so she did not get to scan the island to find the children; however, once they were on land again, she slipped away to use a washroom where she could be alone and unseen for a few minutes.

As she continued checking things out, she and Mike conferred. They decided that the best way to survey the situation physically was for Mike to return and become a security guard. Merle had already determined where the men's changing room was, so it was easy to get Mike dressed up suitably. (He was getting used to having her dress him up!)

Chapter 22

"Hmmm, that's odd!" the sailor muttered, looking at the golden butterfly fluttering around in front of him. "Closest land is twenty miles from here. What the heck is it doing out here?"

He smiled and watched it flutter around, then paid no more mind to it. After all, who would think anything of a butterfly flitting about, even if it is far away from land?

The butterfly flew throughout the ship, even into the interior. Others saw it as well, but it was a butterfly, so who cared? Good thing Papi had not chosen to transition into a bee or a mosquito!

When she had finished, Papi flew off across the water toward the nearest land. (or so they thought!)

***

"And where have you been, little Papi? I am going to have to keep a closer watch on you!" laughed Tarita. "I think calling you Papillon was the right name for you, my little butterfly."

Papi beamed at her idol. She would do anything for Tarita's blessings.

In her little butterfly voice, she said, "I found the children."

"What children are you talking about, Papi?" Tarita asked.

"I knew Merle went to get the children from the bad man, but they were not there on the island; so, I went to find them... and I did."

"How did you know what Merle was doing? There was no general chat about the expedition?" Tarita queried. "Do you know how to do something I do not know about?"

"I love you and Merle so much that I taught myself how to know what you are thinking. When Merle went away, I wanted to know where she was going; so, I read her mind. Then when she did not come back for a long time; I wanted to make sure she was ok. That was when she told me she could not find the children."

Tarita smiled a proud smile at her protégé, and asked, "So how did you find the children?"

"Merle said she could not find them on the island, so I went looking for them. I sensed their energy when Merle thought about them, so it led me to them. They are on a boat. I became my butterfly and flew to the boat to find them."

"When I landed on the boat, a man saw me. He gave me a funny look, it made him laugh to see me. I think he thought I was a real butterfly! Then I continued flying around the boat. I could hear them but could not find them at first. I found them in a cabin at the bottom."

"Where is the boat?" Tarita asked. "Is it far?"

Papi got out an atlas and found the right page. "It is off this coast, heading in this direction." She pointed north on the map.

"Can you contact Merle and tell her?" "She needs to know right away!"

Papi smiled and closed her eyes, then disappeared. There sat a beautiful golden butterfly. She waved her wings at her mentor, then disappeared.

***

Merle was getting very anxious. She knew time was marching by, and that was a bad thing, but she could not find the children or even get a sense of them. Mike had walked over every inch of the property with no result. They were at a loss.

She found a place she could be alone, under a tree, to relax and go inside. A few minutes later, she felt something bumping her face. Startled, she opened her eyes. Before her, a golden butterfly.

"Well, Tarita, this must be important for you to travel all this way! Wait a minute! You are not Tarita. Your markings are different. Are you Papillon?"

Papillon fluttered her wings with recognition. She then landed on the ground, returning to her human form.

She smiled at her beloved Merle, then said, "The children are not here on the island. I found them on a ship. They are going to a place very far from here to be resold. We need to hurry to get them before they land."

Merle knew the place well by now, so they headed to the library. She got an atlas so Papi could show her where the ship had been when she was on board.

"Oh my, Papi, there is no time to waste. I have things I need, so I have to travel the way other people do. Please go back to the ship so I can track you. I will be there as quickly as I can."

There was a small cruiser at the dock, preparing to return to the mainland. Merle waved at the pilot, asking if he could give her a ride.

During the trip, she realized that the boat she was looking for was only a few hours away. Traveling by water would be the fastest way. Now she just needed to convince the pilot to take her there.

It was easy. She just let him enjoy her magical smile one time, and he would do anything she desired! Once they had docked the cruiser and had offloaded the other people, he helped Merle get her supplies. And they were off.

It never occurred to him it might be strange to be running off across the ocean chasing an unknown ship with a person he had only met a couple of hours before.

As they headed out to sea, Merle pondered what cover story she could create to get herself on board, while raising no concerns from the captain.

***

As they raced into range; Merle knew there was only one option. She focused on the pilot's head, connecting with his mind, she suggested he was feeling very dizzy. Almost instantly, he flopped down on the deck, passing right out.

Taking the wheel, she powered closer, calling mayday on the radio. The captain brought the boat to a halt, recognizing that the call had come from the little cruiser near them.

When the captain asked them what the reason for the mayday was. She simply replied that the pilot had passed out for no apparent reason. She needed help because she could not attend to him and drive the boat.

The crew tethered the little boat on the side, then lifted both on board. They escorted the pilot to the medical room while Merle found herself in front of the captain. Perfect!

Within a minute of her arrival, the captain had changed course, heading to the port nearest the Matrix. He did not even seem conscious that he had changed direction.

The captain told her to relax in the lounge while they attended to the pilot. Instead, Merle moved about the ship, searching for the children. As she searched, she set the intention that all people on board were passive towards her and would do as she asked them. This indeed made her job easy!

As they ushered her into the place where they were being held, a little golden butterfly set upon her. The children laughed their heads off as the butterfly continued its antics. Who wouldn't get a little giddy with a butterfly entertaining them with its flips and flutters above their head?

When Merle started speaking to them in their own language, they stopped watching the butterfly, listening to her.

She told them; she was there to rescue them. They would go home with her, and not wherever they had thought, once they had cleared customs. At first, the children were a little wary, but when she told them that the golden butterfly was her friend, they warmed up to her. As she spoke, the butterfly sat still on her shoulder.

It seemed an endless trip, so Merle decided this was a splendid opportunity for them to get a start on some of the very basics they would learn once they were home at the Matrix. The children relaxed, grateful for some positive attention, so they listened and followed her guidance.

Merle contacted Rose to apprise her of the situation. Rose then contacted the immigration authorities to prepare for them.

There was going to be one very unhappy man, or will that be two unhappy men, when they find out the ship never made it to its destination!

Chapter 23

Papillon slept in her little bed that night. She could feel her butterfly wings wrapped around her, so she felt snug as a bug in a rug. She was so tired after her big and exciting expedition.

In her dream, she saw a beautiful angel, who looked down upon her with the most loving eyes. After a moment, the Angel spoke to her, saying, "*I am Rachel. I serve the Universal God that created this earth and all that exists. I invite you to join me in this moment of knowing yourself through the eyes of God.*"

Papillon smiled back at her, even though she was still fast asleep.

"*I speak to you tonight to commend you on the splendid work you did today, however, you need to learn a most important lesson to ensure your personal growth measures up with your skill as a butterfly. Listen when Bethany counsels you on the morrow.*" And with those words, Rachel faded away as Papi fell into a deep sleep.

As Papi slept, she dreamed of an enormous snake curled up in her belly. She watched it unwind and reach up towards her head. She was not afraid, just curious why a snake would be inside her. The snake worked its way up until it stretched its body so far that its head poked right out the top of her head. Even though she was sleeping; she laughed and laughed at the silliness of the snake.

***

At breakfast that morning, Beth did indeed seek out Papillon. Beth smiled at her and gave her the biggest hug Papi had ever enjoyed.

"You did something well beyond your age yesterday, my Papillon! Because of you, we could rescue those children. You have an amazing gift," Beth praised her. "After break this morning, I want you to meet me out in the backyard. Because of your splendid work yesterday, we feel you require some extra training, so you can be even better at what you are so capable of doing."

Later in the morning, after the break, Papi strolled out to the backyard. As she arrived, so did Beth. Beth asked her to walk into the forest with her.

"I need to ask you what made you take on the job you did yesterday. What you did was far beyond your age."

"I could feel how scared the children were, so I wanted to help them," she said almost apologetically.

"And how did you feel when you became your butterfly?" Beth continued with her inquiry.

"Scared and angry. It reminded me how I felt when I first learned to be a butterfly at home."

"That is what we figured. The lessons we will start today are lessons that will continue for many years, in fact, likely for the rest of your life. You learned this skill out of fear for your own safety. That is why you sensed the fear in the children. We have training that will help you reframe the old beliefs that caused you to choose to become a butterfly when you were still back home, so you can be an even more amazing butterfly but based in Absolute Love."

"Why do I need to do this if I can already become a butterfly anytime I want, Beth?"

Beth turned and gave Papi a big hug, then she reassured her, saying, "You have done nothing wrong, so please take this as only an opportunity to become an even better butterfly."

"The energy you use now to become a butterfly is based in fear. If you continue to transition using the energy of fear, it will either break down your ability to become a butterfly at will or it will affect your health. We need to help you clear the fear from your beliefs and replace it with Universal Love or Divine Love, so you are acting in the Power of God. Do you understand, Papi?"

"Do you want to be the most amazing butterfly ever?" Beth comforted her.

"Better than Tarita?"

"No. Not better than Tarita. Part of working in Love is that we do not compare ourselves. Tarita is already a pretty amazing butterfly in her own way. You will have your special way too. In fact, Tarita is going to help you."

And at that moment, Tarita joined them and gave them both a big hug.

She smiled at Papi and said to her, "You have shown you are already a great butterfly. I am looking forward to helping you become even better. Maybe we will have some work to do together once you have mastered your skill from the essence of love."

"I am going to work really hard because I want to work with you, Tarita. I have a question though if I may."

Beth looked at her and held her hand out to encourage her to ask the question.

"Last night an angel came to me in my sleep. She told me about this meeting today. After she left, I had a dream where I saw a big snake in my belly. At first, it was just lying there relaxing, then soon it began lifting its head, traveling up my back until it finally stuck its head out the top of my head. What does that mean?"

"The Angel that visited you, we call Rachel. She is the guiding force that created The Matrix. You are very special and fortunate that Rachel came to speak with you alone. It must have been because of the fine work you did yesterday." Tarita smiled at her proudly.

"I assume Rachel gave you the dream about the snake. The snake symbolizes the sleeping energy that rests in the tailbone of all humans. When the snake traveled up your back and out your head, it was symbolic of what we call Kundalini Energy, a powerful energy that truly connects you with Source.

I would say that it was a message to all of us that we need to start your training by teaching you how to work with this energy. It will make you much stronger so you can hold yourself in butterfly longer and better."

Beth then looked at Papi and said, "I think this is enough for now, Papillon. I think you should sit in the forest for a little while just to soak up some wonderful earth energy, then head off to your classes."

"Meet me here after the afternoon break and we will begin learning the Kundalini. This is going to be exciting."

***

Early in the afternoon, the children were outside practicing being trees and other plants, when all at once, there was yelling. Sheila was leading the class, but she was looking in a different direction when the yelling began. She turned around quickly to see Papillon and another girl yelling at each other.

Leaving the other children to continue their playing as she walked over to the distressed girls. She looked at both of them, not understanding the issue, then took a deep breath, trying to size up what had caused this interruption.

She looked at both girls, asking, "What is the problem, girls? This is highly unusual for you to act this way. We always try to talk out our differences rather than yelling like this."

The other girl replied first, "Papi says she is special and is better than us. I told her she was not. Papi got mad and started yelling at me."

"Papi, is this true what she says?" Sheila continued.

"Beth and Tarita told me I was special because Rachel came to sce me in my dream last night."

"You do have a special gift. Because of your gift, Rachel needed to speak with you. This indeed is a great honor for you; however, she did not mean you were any different from the other children... or even any of the staff. In fact, because of your talent, it has given you a much larger workload.

Every person anywhere is special, and we are all equal. You will learn through your training that when people believe they are better than others, deep inside, they believe they are not as good. So please apologize to your friend and give her a big hug. Let's continue with our play."

***

For many months Papi tried hard to curb the angst she felt inside herself. She was diligent in doing her exercises; she spent as much time as she could communing with nature, but the unsettling feelings only grew larger. It did not like the idea that Papi was trying to kill it.

Papi struggled, and it got the best of her. One day, during a walk in the woods, she lost control of herself. It was late spring; and so, the garden was already planted and growing. As she walked, trying to calm the monster inside her, she saw the garden with all the pretty flowers shining their beautiful heads to the sun.

She ran into the garden, thrashing about like a mad man, pulling the flowering plants out of the ground. There was no one around to stop her. The rage just grew greater and greater. She could not stop herself until the entire garden was in ruins. Papi then melted, sobbing as she became unconscious, lying on the ground.

As she slept, Rachel came to visit her once again.

"My dearest Papillon, the war inside you is so great; too great for such a young person to endure. I will help you. Please look into my eyes."

Papi knew this was a major event because she had been told that no one ever looked into an Angel's eyes; the power was just too great. Papi did as requested, though, peering into her eyes.

A pleasant rush of great peace poured into her every cell. Her whole being became very placid... for about one minute.

The part of her that held the great anger inside her burst out. In her mind, Papi began lashing out at Rachel, screaming like a wounded beast. Rachel smiled at Papi and continued staring into her eyes with a peaceful look of love, like a mother shares with her child.

Rachel took a deep breath, holding it for a moment, then blew the air right into Papi's face. The anger dissolved.

She whispered to the child, "*The part of you that is feeling so much anger is trying to protect you. It still sees the world as being unsafe. I call to this part to know and accept that the danger is past, now and forever. You are safe, my beloved.*"

***

Rose could feel what was happening in the garden, so she grabbed Tomas and ran out to help. As they arrived at the garden, they came to a crashing halt when they saw all the destruction. Not one flower remained standing!

At first, they did not see Papi. Searching every inch, they found the little imp at the edge of the garden, crumpled into a little lump. They found the child breathing, but unconscious. As Tomas picked the tiny girl up to carry her back inside, Rose smiled that same smile as Rachel, then waved her hand over the garden. The flowers obeyed, healing themselves to their former splendor.

***

Papi slept for what seemed like days. Tarita attended to her while she slept. It was a deep sleep, more like a coma. This had been a life shattering event for the little girl. They could only hope now that she would recover.

She woke after four days. She lay still, opening her eyes long enough to let her nurse know she was back; but she did not speak or make any attempt to communicate.

Tarita brought her soup and helped her to sit up so she could eat. Once she had eaten the soup, Papi looked a little more alive, but she remained motionless, almost trancelike.

Tarita sought out Rose. Rose suggested that this might require some special butterfly medicine.

Tarita knew in an instant what she needed to do. As Papi lay down to sleep again, she saw a beautiful golden butterfly flying above her, showering her with wonderful butterfly dust. She knew then that she must return to the land of the living.

Chapter 24

Mike and Tomas had worked for a long, what seemed like a never-ending time. Rescuing children was a very meticulous and arduous task. There just was no room for error with so many little lives at stake.

The men had settled back into life at the Matrix. They began right away working with the six special boys from the first group. These boys had been living at the Matrix for a long time now, so they were well settled in and used to the daily routines.

It was very fortunate that the boys had never been to school beforehand. They were also young enough that they knew little about the world or about human beings. All they had known in their young lives was extreme terror.

Mike reminisced for a few moments about his own traumatized childhood. He could never verbalize how grateful he was for Merle coming forward to protect him from his father. Her choice that day through expressing this dynamic energy reshaped their lives, creating a life expression beyond belief.

He also thought about how it had transformed the relationships he had with other children after he knew how to use it. Bullies became friends while strangers warmed up to him and accepted him as the wonderful, sensitive person he enjoyed being.

Living at the Matrix, the tools they needed for them to process the lessons of their young lives were now well in place, so the boys were now pretty normal as far as their ability to live life in a more than functional manner.

Only these boys were not normal boys. They were the ones who claimed they could feel kicking inside their bodies back in the early days of their time at the Matrix. It was now time for Mike and Tomas to begin the long process of bringing these boys up to speed about the truth of who they are. This would not be any quick chat about the facts of life. No, this was going to be a long and precise process that would take up to two years.

Sheila had already introduced them to the concept that all humans carry aspects of both masculine and feminine energies, but now they needed to learn the next level about their own truth.

The first thing that Mike and Tomas wanted to do, though, was having some guy time. This was just as much for them as for the boys. After all the pressure of the rescues, as well as spending so much time in their female personages, it was time to get grounded in male energy for a while.

So, what could they do to foster a little testosterone and male bonding?

Merle, the always go-to person for figuring things out, had the answer right away. (Besides, it was something she had always wanted to do as well... and she wouldn't have to do all the work!)

Rock climbing!

And this was not just climbing on a bunch of rocks, this was serious up the mountain, hanging off the wall, rock climbing!

Near to their town was a mountaineering school. This was the perfect venue for the men and the boys to blow off some steam and get that male hormone kicking in, so Mike registered all six of the boys and the two men. (Ladies ride for free!)

Not so many days later, they all found themselves learning the basics of an absolute, testosterone-pumping sport. There was not one boy or man present who was anything less than 100% into this project. To be perfectly honest, the boys, as much as they enjoyed playing yoga, it just was not scary enough... yah... it's a guy thing!

The instructors all wanted to ensure that the boys enjoyed themselves while being safe. After all, they were soon going to be hanging off cliff walls... not your typical Sunday afternoon stroll!

Once everyone was outfitted, they started off doing simpler things like hiking. Even a sport like hiking has specific rules for doing the sport well, so everyone gets to go home at night.

Up hills and down hills, they trekked around the locale of the school. Some trails were tricky, so the boys had to figure out how to manage obstacles in their way. One trail even had a narrow passage they had to traverse along a bluff that was only wide enough for one skinny kid! Mike, even though he was not considered a big person, had to traverse this section with his back against the wall just because he was too big to walk forward! Good thing no backpack!

A couple weeks of hiking around local trails showed how serious these boys were in learning this new craft, so the instructors decided it was time for all of them to begin serious rock climbing. One day in class to introduce them all to the equipment, climbing etiquette, and the safety rules, everyone was ready to rock (but not roll).

Mike fretted a bit about Tomas. He never acted in an overly masculine way, but he had certainly proved himself in playing his part with the motorcycle gang... but then who could be a man's man when they have a female inside them, who is a living butterfly!

Mike's mother henning proved to be unfounded, though. Tomas took to climbing like he was born to do it. He did later confide to Mike that he had spoken with Tarita and she agreed that if things got too scary for either of them, she would automatically take over and turn them into a butterfly. How's that for a safety mechanism!

Mike chuckled as he wondered what the instructors would think and do if they saw Tomas turn into a butterfly!

The training hill was only about one hundred feet high, and it gently sloped inward, making the climb somewhat easier than what they would face in the future. What was most important was that it gave them a great location where they could safely practice their craft without Tomas needing to become a butterfly! (He never heard the end of that!)

For the next few months, as long as the weather cooperated, the gang was out at the school or at other local sites that provided bigger and bigger challenges. Mike made sure he did not get too wrapped up in his own learning and his own need for a testosterone fix so that he could observe and make notes about each of the boys.

He felt he needed to understand how each one of them was progressing, not only as a climber, but how they were maturing as males. They would need a good base of male energy to emerge into the amazing people they were soon to become.

***

It was becoming apparent that sooner than later was the timeline for having the talks with the boys. This would not be a simple bedside chat with a young child. This was going to be more like the Ostriches and Grasshoppers... or ... something much bigger anyway!

Beth noticed during her visits to the classes that some boys were getting typical pre-pubertal symptoms, such as crackling voices and shards of hair on their faces. There was definitely no time to waste now... and it was Mike's job to bring them up to speed!

Mike thought that the best way to start this was to practice some inner "get to know me" work. That way, they could become more familiar with what goes on inside these special bodies.

Before he could even begin the process, one boy put up his hand. "Mike, we have been talking amongst ourselves and we would like to discuss something that is going on, especially for us older guys."

"Go ahead," Mike invited, thinking this was some kind of stall. No such luck!

"We seem to have these recurring dreams where we are each sitting chatting with a girl who looks just like ourselves. Do we have sisters somewhere we don't know about? How come they talk to us when we are asleep?"

Mike gulped, realizing that the first lesson just jumped from beginner to advanced level, all in one inquiry.

"Boy, you guys don't give a guy a chance to hedge his way into a subject, do you? Okay, here goes everything!"

"As Sheila had told you in an earlier session; all humans have both male and female aspects to them. The female aspect is the passive side, so when you are nurturing yourself... or someone else, that would be female energy or when you take the time to enjoy beauty. There are a lot more feminine energy things you do without thinking about it, but those are just good examples.

Male energy is action-based like when we rock climb. These energies have nothing to do with the gender of the body of the person who is doing whichever. It just is a way of separating the two types of activities. The soul, which is the true infinite part of us, does not have a gender. One lifetime, you might be male, in another, you might be female, but each time it is still you. You just incarnate into the body that suits the lessons of that lifetime best.

The reason you boys have become a distinct group is that you all have said to have something that kicks you from the inside, right?"

They all nodded in agreement as they felt little kicks coming from their insides.

"Until the last few years, all the people who live on our planet belonged to a species called Homo Sapiens. Before that, there were Neanderthals, The Cro-Magnons, and several others. Recently, at least in the great span of time, a new species has appeared to share the earth with the Homo Sapiens. We call ourselves Homo integratis."

Mike stopped again to let that piece sink in. Then he added. "We, as in everybody in this room... are all members of this new species."

The boys sat there, waiting for him to continue. Mike had expected a flurry of questions, but all he got was looks of expectancy for him to continue.

"Homo sapiens are born into either a male or a female body. Homo integratis, both male and female, carry the attributes of both genders in equal proportions on any levels, including physical. The reason this is important is that males and females, even in Homo sapiens, communicate and process information differently. Homo integratis incorporate and function in both. Double the magic!

Again, still expecting to be interrupted by questions. No such luck!

"We are going to start training you now so that you can meet and work with your female selves. The girl you chatted with in your dream is not your sister... she is your female alter ego or your female counterpart. She is the one who has been kicking you all these years. She was just telling you she is there. Once you have completed maturing, she will show herself."

At that, each of the boys felt not one kick, but almost like a drum roll coming from inside.

Mike was sure this time there would be a flurry of questions... still none. The boys just kept listening.

Mike then looked at Tomas, shrugged his shoulders. In the blink of an eye, Merle and Tarita were standing in front of the boys!

Now the boys were excited!

"We're going to be able to do that? Wow! That's cool!"

Mike and Tomas returned to continue the conversation. This was going to be way easier than they had ever thought. Guess it pays when you get people who don't know this is not the way regular kids act. (whatever that is!)

"Yes, at some point, once you have matured into your adult body, you will be able to do this, too. The advantage is that it allows you to function more completely in either female or male energy, and in time, you will work with both energies at the same time.

This is part of the reason we have excelled in finding and rescuing the other children. We use both sides of our being equally well, and now that we have fully integrated, we decide together which expression will give us the greatest chance of success during a project," Mike finished... or so he thought.

Another boy then asked, "How come there are no girls in this group? Aren't any of them Homo integratis?"

Tomas decided it was time for Mike to have a break, so he jumped in.

"I will take this, Mike. Let me have some fun too!"

"There are female based Homo integratis, as well as male. They are quite different, though. They serve different purposes in the unfolding of our new species.

The Universe has deemed the members who are born into male bodies are to play a more active role in carrying out earth-based projects. Our role at this time is to locate other members, then bring them to centers such as The Matrix. This supports them in learning about themselves so they become fully empowered members of Homo integratis.

There are many, many more of us out there that need to be found and self-discovered.

Those born into female bodies serve a different purpose. Their work is in nurturing the new members, assisting them in their own personal healing and in spiritual growth. They have an equal male with them. However, there has not yet been any need for them to transition into a male expression. Female Homo

Sapiens, our forerunners, integrated their male sides a long time ago, so it functions adequately without having to give it physical expression.

Most of the staff here at the Matrix are Homo integratis. It is a natural part of who we are. You don't see us change from one aspect to the other because we do not mean it to be for show. We only change when we need to.

I was a member of the staff when I discovered I was Homo integratis, or more correctly, Tarita decided she needed to appear because she was tired of me not letting her be a part of my life. I was much older than when Mike first, albeit unconsciously, met Merle.

My life had been like Mike's, only it was my mother who was the problem for me. She used to leave me for many days when she would go off on drunken binges. My father would go away trying to find her, then he would bring her back and beat her. It was a never-ending cycle. We went hungry so much of the time. If we complained, it was our turn to be beat. My sisters and I were terrified all the time, so we all became too afraid to be seen. When our grandmother intervened, she rescued us and took us away. Like you fellows, Mike and I have both grown up in traumatic environments that supported us, becoming who we are today.

It was right in the cafeteria that Tarita first joined us, and I cannot tell you how it pleases me to share this amazing life with her.

The female members each also have special abilities unique to their life purpose. It is one of the most important tasks we have here, which is to help them find and develop that... or those unique skills. I am extra lucky because I have such a strong female side that I have one of those unique female skills as well... or should I say more correctly... Tarita does."

And at that Tarita appeared and... became her golden butterfly!

Chapter 25

Tomas woke with a start. It felt like someone was poking him. When he opened his eyes, Rachel was hovering above him, waiting for him to regain consciousness.

"*Good day, my beloved Thomas. I have an important mission for you to attend to today. You must leave to complete it right away.*"

Tomas sat up, rubbing his eyes, trying to make sense of what had just happened. He looked at Rachel and waited for her to continue.

"*As a rescuer, we sometimes have missions that are not rescuing children. This is one we need to deal with it right away, as its completion is imperative to the health of our Mother Earth.*

If we wait too long, it could cause an earth-ending catastrophe. We need it to be stopped so that the evolution of earth's citizens can complete in a timely manner.

A drilling company is working in an arctic region where the earth's surface is thin. If they puncture the protective barrier below the surface, it would expose the contents to the earth's atmosphere, creating an explosion and causing the planet to shatter.

The owners of the company have been told to stop drilling, but are ignoring the order, justifying that the order came not from a recognized authority.

Please get there and stop the work before the drills break through the protective layer, with or without the approval of the supervisors."

***

This is a moment when it is an advantage, such as in a case like today's, to have wings to do your own flying with. However, the arctic was much too far for even a Golden Butterfly to travel in a short time. What They did not know was that Rachel had invoked a special new skill into their consciousness.

"How the heck am I supposed to get to the Arctic to save the planet?" fretted Tomas.

Tarita just laughed and fluttered her wings. In an instant, they were sitting on the roof of a building at the worksite!

As they sat looking at the beautiful sight that was being marred by the certain destruction of our beloved planet, they decided the workers would be more likely to listen to Tarita.

Tarita strolled up to the drilling rig and waited until someone noticed her. The man who saw her first stared at her like he was looking at a ghost.

"Well, little lady, what are you doing way out here? We don't get guests very often."

Tarita smiled at him and waved her hand, doing her trusty transition symbol. The man stopped what he was doing and sat down. She then walked into the rig's work area and continued to project her transition energy.

The rig came to a grinding halt as he walked away, sounding like it had hit a giant granite boulder. Smoke spewed from the top of the drill as it stopped. As Tarita continued wandering through the site looking for people, she watched as they each complied with the force of the energy on their consciousness.

Before long, they all moved into the lunchroom, where Tarita joined them. As she entered, there was a loud angry voice screaming through the two-way radio sitting on the desk at one end of the room.

The owner of the voice wanted to know why the machine had stopped... And when it would be back up and running again. No one replied to the voice. They all just sat there, looking at each other, then at Tarita.

She walked up to the front of the room and introduced herself. "I am Tarita. The work you are doing at this site is endangering the planet, so the highest authority has instructed me to have you end your work.

Your drill is pushing toward a thin protective layer. Damaging it will cause a cataclysmic event, so great that the earth itself will explode into pieces."

She pressed on as the men listened and absorbed her every word.

"It is necessary that you proceed now to remove your equipment from this location. We have provided your supervisors with the documentation to guide you on where to move your site to. So far, they have refused to comply. I have been instructed to appear before you to enforce this action."

Tarita then smiled again and repeated the symbol with her hand. The men stood up and cheered her, feeling relieved that they had realized their suspicions.

With no further discussion needed, the men began tearing down the camp. Disconnecting the two-way radio was first!

Tarita waited for the job to be completed. Once they had loaded all the equipment onto trucks and readied for the journey away from the current site, Tarita told the job supervisor where the new location was.

On completion, Tarita closed the energy on the area then Rachel placed an energetic wall throughout the region, thus preventing any further intrusions.

The supervisor offered Tarita a ride, but she just smiled and fluttered off (just for effect!)

After the fact:

After the employees dropped off the equipment at the new site, they all opted to quit, so they could be at home with their families.

The supervisor that offered Tarita a ride decided he should become a Buddhist Monk after seeing a miracle, so he bought a one-way ticket to Tibet!

Chapter 26

"There is no such thing as normal in our world," Mike said to the boys as they began their morning lessons. "Everyone is uniquely different. In fact, we are all in constant change as we progress through our lives.

The only thing that should ever feel normal is how wonderful it feels to be yourself and your love for life. By learning how to listen to your thoughts and how you feel as you progress through each moment, you will continue to learn about yourself and progress as your own normal.

All the staff and children who live here at Matrix have had extensive training from day one to be part of the process of getting to know themselves. As well as accepting that every one of us is special in our own way, we must support and assist each other in learning how to love ourselves as the unique individuals we each are.

It is important for each of you fellows to feel safe and confident enough to explore how you feel as you mature into your adult beings, and be able to reach out to your leaders for help when concerns arise."

Mike was not usually this long-winded, but this lesson was of great importance. The boys needed to each embrace the person who they express themselves as; especially once their female aspect showed herself. Ridicule and embarrassment had no room in this!

"All of you have come from challenging and traumatic backgrounds. It is amazing that you are even alive, never mind prospering and thriving as the powerhouses you are and are becoming. Our program has provided each of you with the tools to clear the dysfunctional beliefs that you learned in your childhood; and now today you stand clear, ready, and able to accept the adult version of you.

You will each mature and take on your full nature in your own time. Only the Cosmic knows when that will happen. It is essential that you all support each other now and always. The group sitting here today will be your group for all time. You have developed relationships with each other that started even before you arrived here at the Matrix. If there are any of your gang that you have not bonded with, or you have issues with, this is the time to clear these issues. Everybody has each other's backs. Are there questions?"

One boy raised his hand, asking, "Are you and Tomas always going to be our leaders?"

"Great question! Tomas and I will always be a part of this group. However, we are not really your leaders per se; we are your guides.

There may be projects where you fellows will take part in that Tomas and I may not. There may even be times where you will work with Beth or Rose or other females... and then he laughed as he felt a kick in his side... don't let me forget Merle and Tarita!

We each take counsel through our Blessed Angel Rachel. She, and only she, understands the needs for each project as it comes along. Case in point, the project that Tomas and Tarita just completed stopping the drilling rigs up in the Arctic.

This is a very exciting life you have chosen. We hope the training we have given you and continue to provide will support you with the tools so that safety and success are always yours.

The most important asset you possess is your mind. If you believe that safety is yours, because it is part of your universal design, you can access and employ your unique skills, providing you with success in any endeavor you choose."

***

This turned out to be a timely talk because not long after it, Beth pointed out again to Mike that more and more of the boys were verging on puberty.

They helped with the oncoming changes by introducing a regimen of extra vitamins and supplements for each of them, as well as extended visualization processes to ensure clarity and self-acceptance along with... of course... generous helpings of rock climbing!

It was decided that a closer watch needed to be kept on each boy to monitor his maturing process and to ensure that he received the greatest of support in every way so that when he had matured, he was ready, willing, and able to function in his most full capacity. They also decided that the boys should keep to themselves in their group until all of them had completed the maturing process. At the rate these guys accept things, this would only take a few months.

It was fortunate for these boys that they were being provided for like this. Mike and Tomas were adamant about being there for each and all of them, as they did not want them to have to go through the process the way they had to do so, so many years before.

***

A couple of days after Mike's big talk, he and Tomas were sitting around during a break with the boys when one of them asked if they could continue the earlier chat. They wanted to speak to it.

Tomas responded by pulling his and Mike's chairs to face the boys, forming a circle.

When they had all settled in, he began. "We have been talking amongst ourselves since your talk the other day. Although we don't understand what is going to happen to us when we have completed maturity, we know we are unified as a group and are excited about getting to do some projects like you fellows have been doing.

We have also decided that since we will have an easier time in getting to know our female aspects, we have decided that we are all changing our names."

Both men looked at him, then scanned the other boys for confirmation. It was easy to see there was complete agreement in the air. The boys sat proud as peacocks.

"Well, this is going to be interesting," Tomas said, motioning for him to continue.

"Since we will be able to transition easily between our two personas, we have decided that instead of having to have one name for each half like you guys, we are all adopting a single name for our unified person. The names will be neither male nor female... But the names of birds!"

At that, the boys jumped up and down, hooting and hollering, celebrating their decision.

Mike looked at them. "Well, don't keep us in suspense. Let's hear what you have decided."

The boy who had been talking introduced himself before he let the others take their turns, moving from one chair to the next.

"I am Condor. My name symbolizes leadership, wisdom, justice, and goodness."

The boy beside him then rose. "I am Goose. My name symbolizes fearlessness and bravery!"

"I am Hummingbird," the next boy said, jumping up so fast he almost knocked over Goose. "My name symbolizes love, joy, and good luck. These birds are healers and deliverers of love.... and they fly really fast."

Following suit, the next boy stood, looking at Mike and Tomas with a stern look. "I am Raven. The Raven purveys wisdom and light."

The next boy, taking his turn. "I am Phoenix. My bird represents fresh starts, transformation, an undefeatable spirit, and immortality. I think all of us could hold this name!"

To round things off, the boy next to Mike stood up, walked to the center of the circle, slowly looking around at each of them. "I am Falcon! My bird symbolizes vision, protection, and wisdom."

Then he continued, "We each believe the bird we have chosen represents who we have both become and intend to be as full members of our group, The Wind Surfers!"

At that, the boys started dancing around yelling 'Wind Surfers' over and over again. In fact, they made so much noise that Rose and the other girls came running in to find out what all the hooting and hollering was about.

Tomas turned to the ladies and without hesitation introduced each of the boys by their new name and then introduced The Wind Surfers!

The girls gave them a round of applause and congratulated them for their excellent choices. After they left, the boys were feeling so elated they all decided a good hike was in order so they could work off the excitement.

A few days later, when the boys returned to their rooms, they found T-shirts laying on their beds with their new name emblazoned on the front and Wind Surfers on the back.

There would be no holding these boys back now!

***

A big surprise happened when the shirts were being handed out. There was a new member in the Wind Surfers!

All the children were doing their yoga exercises as they did every morning. There were not so many children at the center these days, as so many of the second intake had been adopted out. In fact, there was only one person from the second group in the room, and only because she had chosen not to be adopted out.

Can you guess who?

Of course, it was none other than Papi!

She thought to herself, "Why on earth would I want to be adopted out so that I would have to live in a house with regular people and go to regular school and all that other regular stuff? My home and my people are here!"

Papi was already in the studio when the boys trundled in, sitting in Lotus position, meditating. Absolute bliss radiated from her as the boys admired how far she had come since her crash.

The boys looked at her, then looked at each other, all smiling with approval. They all felt the special connection during yoga, so right after the session was over, as Papi was heading to the breakroom, Hummingbird sidled up beside her.

She smiled at him and called him by his old name. He said to her, "Many important things have happened since we last met. We are glad you have recovered and that you have stayed with us at Matrix."

She smiled again, not knowing what was coming next. Hummingbird continued, "The six of us boys have been working together as a group now for many months. Mike and Tomas are helping us to build a strong bond with everyone in the group so that when we do projects together, we know we have the support of each other."

He paused as they walked, then placed his hand on Papi's arm to stop her. He looked at her straight in the eyes, saying, "all of us agree we are missing a member of our group... You, Papi."

She looked blankly at him, then started crying in joy. Then she said, "I have watched you guys for so long, wishing I were a boy so I could be a part of your group. Thank you! You have made my day... No! You have made my life!"

When they walked into the break room, the other boys were sitting together. Hummingbird sat down in his seat, then Raven pushed out a chair and waved his arm to Papi, inviting her to sit down.

When Mike and Tomas joined them later to start their next class, it was a pleasant surprise to see this tiny little wisp of a girl. Papi had joined the boys.

Mike commented, "I see we have a guest today. Welcome, Papi."

Hummingbird stood up and said to Mike, "Good morning, Mike and Tomas. Papi is not a guest. She is now a full-fledged member of The Wind Surfers. We feel she has proven that she will be a valuable member of our group. Since she has chosen not to be adopted out, we all agreed that she should be one of us."

Tomas then said. "Well. I guess we had better put Papi through her paces then and see if she can keep up with us. First on the agenda is some hiking and rock climbing. Think you are up to it, Papi? Oh, and no cheating by flying to the top of the hill, okay?"

Raven got up and walked over to a large closet and reached inside. He then walked over to Papi and presented her with her own hiking and climbing gear.

He looked at her beaming an enormous smile and said, "We were expecting this to happen!"

So, the Wind Surfers were now 7!

Chapter 27

The authorities finally released the third intake of children. They could join the fun at the Matrix. The situation was prolonged because the people to whom they had been intended had applied to stop the Matrix staff from aborting their purchase of the children.

These people claimed they operated a mission that took in war orphans They would provide families for them almost as soon as they would arrive. However, they were sorely stilted when the regulators investigated, discovering that the families that would raise them were not families at all. The children would become slaves if they gave the original claimants approval.

This situation was not over, by any means. The original claimants made a vow to reclaim their properties, despite what the authorities had decided, even though the children were now safely nestled into the Matrix.

***

The entire process had been grueling for these children. Exhausted and anxious when they arrived at the Center, they had no idea what to expect since no one from the Matrix could visit them during their incarceration.

To ease their worries once they were all sitting in the cafeteria, they enjoyed a wonderful surprise! A beautiful golden butterfly flitted into the room. Pardon me! Two beautiful Golden butterflies flitted into the room!

The children recognized the first Golden Butterfly as the one that had visited them on the boat. Soon, they were all relaxed, giggling as the butterflies chased each other and played little butterfly games for them.

By the time Rose came into the room to start the intake process, they were all relaxed and smiling. The two butterflies flew out of the room to allow her to have the complete attention of the children.

Rose beamed at the children. Her heart was ready to explode from the love she felt for them. She invited the others in to meet their new children. Before any of the adults joined the children, they set their energy so that it was really big, friendly, and full of love, so that when they entered, the children could feel the positive effects.

They now had adopted all the first two groups of children out into families in the community except the members (all seven) of the Wind Surfers. They had chosen to be permanent residents of the Matrix. This meant there were plenty of rooms to be filled with soon-to-be happy children.

This would be the first invocation where the Wind Surfers would take part in the retraining. Rose introduced them once the adults had finished their introductions. It thrilled the new children to see some people near their own age. The looks on their faces relaxed when Rose told the children that all these children had been rescued from a similar situation.

The Wind Surfers then merged into the audience to begin the process of inclusion.

***

For the next couple of days, there were no intense instructions, as Rose wanted to give all the children a chance to sleep, get their lives organized, and get to know their new friends. Papi and her gang continued with their own routines as much as possible, including their morning yoga and meditation. They left the doors open for the new children to see what they were doing... and to allow them to join if they chose.

The break room was the fullest it had been in a very long time. Rose had the kitchen staff bake some special bread so that the air was drenched with the yummy flavor. Who could resist?

Radiant smiles replaced the bread in a heartbeat. Oh, that bread tasted so good, especially with butter and homemade strawberry jam... and what child could refuse a steamy hot cup of cocoa?

With happy tummies all around, Beth, Sheila, and Teesha led the children outside into the backyard. Today, they were to begin learning concepts of self-knowledge and self-awareness. Where better place to be immersed?

At first, they just let the children look around, but then they gathered them all together to take them into their forest. Soon, she invited each of them to sit down and lean against a tree and enjoy.

Once they looked relaxed enough, Beth invited them to focus on their own breathing for a few moments. She then told them that the trees had a special gift for them. It did not take long before they could feel the loving energy of the cedar trees expanding around them. It felt like the trees were giving them a big hug. All the children accepted the amazing feeling. (Cedar trees like to share hugs with humans, if the humans will give them a chance.)

Beth took them deeper into the quiet.

"Imagine yourself as a drop of water. Feel what it is like to be this little drop. Now let yourself be absorbed into the earth, flowing easily down, down, down.

As you flow down you are absorbed by a little tree root. There are millions of little water drops like you, now flowing up the root, beginning your journey up the tree.

Feel yourself journeying up inside the tree. The nutrients you carry being absorbed into the wood of the tree. Up, up, up you go.

Finally, you find yourself in a leaf of the tree. You can see the sky far off. You look down to the ground. It is very far, but you are a drop of water, so you just enjoy being part of the tree.

Soon you evaporate from the tree leaf and find yourself floating up into the sky. Up, up, up you float until you are absorbed into a fluffy little cloud.

You float along in the sky as more and more little water drops are absorbed into the cloud. The cloud is not so tiny or fluffy anymore. It has become so full of waterdrops that it is now really big and black until finally, it becomes too full.

It lets you go, so you float back down to the earth to repeat the process.

Landing back on the ground, you slip into the roots of your tree, and lift like an elevator right back to the spot where you have been sitting all the time".

After a few minutes, each of them opened their eyes and smiled as they began a new life.

Chapter 28

Rose called the team together once she received the news. This was the first time there had been a problem they could not resolve on their own.

The people who had claimed rights to these children would not let go. They had filed a writ in the Supreme Court claiming that associates of the Matrix had illegally boarded the ship and commandeered it. If they found this to be the case, there could be criminal charges brought forward.

The judge, seeing the case, ordered a Cease and Desist order against the staff at the Matrix regarding any retraining of the children that was not endorsed by the claimants.

This was a disaster!

Once all the key members of the staff were present, Rose called on Rachel.

Rachel appeared in all her splendor, as usual, looked at each of them for a moment. "*Greetings all. I realize the sadness and concern on your faces. Do not fret, for this is another lesson in life for you to embrace.*

You must maintain your power and your clarity throughout this process. This offers great opportunities for all to grow. Remember that we must learn some lessons on the earth plane. They are the most valuable lessons because they offer the greatest opportunity for growth. You could use your metaphysical powers to disburse this problem, but it would just rise again at another time."

Once Rachel had gone, they dug in to find the solution. Before there was a chance to even discuss the matter, there was a knock on the office door. When Mike opened the door, one staffer was standing there with three very officious-looking people.

She said, "These people claim they are from the Bureau of Children. They are here to discuss the matter of the custody of the children in question. They also want to have a look at the premises to determine if it is suitable for the children to be housed here during the trial."

Rose came to the door. "Please come in. We have seats available, and all the board is here, so we might as well have our meeting right now if you wish. Would you like some coffee or tea or water?"

The three government people crept into the room. They were not used to people being considerate to them in such cases. They felt warm and felt the need to remove their jackets. As they sat, they felt relaxed, just about like being at home. Indeed, they will have tea!

The government's efforts to find suitable housing for all the children had failed miserably, so they would not apprehend the children, as they had no place to take them. They had a list of rules that were to be upheld until the trial could happen; likely in about two years. As long as they obeyed the rules, they would leave the children in this residence. They also stated they would make impromptu visits to ensure compliance.

Was that baked bread they smelled? Rose smiled as she increased the power of her projection.

"If we are through with the formal discussions, let's go for a walk around the premises so you can see the quality of lifestyle we provide for the children," Rose said.

So, they formed a convoy, and off the entire group went to see what they could see. The first stop was the cafeteria, where, sure enough, there was fresh bread baking in the oven. That left everyone salivating!

"We can come back here for refreshments after the tour, if you like, I am sure you will have more to discuss!"

They visited the classrooms and the exercise rooms first, then up to the children's residences. All the rooms were clean and neat. Beth and Sheila opened the dresser drawers and closets to show them the amount and quality of clothing the children had. No uniforms or hand-me-downs here!

Their last stop was the residences of the board members and the rooms of the supervisors on the children's wing.

"It impressed us with your operation and your candor. There is no need for the children to be apprehended, as we feel having them here is the best for them. Let's discuss some of the programs you offer while we are sitting in the cafeteria," the lead woman smiled as she licked her lips.

Rose explained that the primary focus at the center was to provide the children with tools to help them heal from the severe trauma from their earlier lives. They also learned to do yoga and meditate. Their mental, physical, emotional, and spiritual well-being were all provided for at the Matrix.

After a wonderful taste of fresh-baked bread and that unique and wonderful tea Rose insisted they drink, all three members left, not exactly sure where they had been.

As they were leaving, the spokesperson for the group said to them, "We will be seeing you soon!" as she shook her head, telling her no, they won't.

***

Once the government people had left, they reconvened in the boardroom. This was getting to be serious business and needed to be handled now... and correctly!

Rose said she knew of a lawyer in town that would be good to handle this situation, so she contacted his secretary and set up a meeting. That afternoon, Rose met with him.

She briefed him on the situation and what had happened that morning.

"We cannot let this case drag on. The judge has set the date for about two years from now. There may be a lot of children that need rescuing during that time, so we just need to nip this problem in the bud. It just is not fair that our good work be limited by such unscrupulous people," Rose started in.

"We have the funds to create a vigorous defense, so I am asking you to prepare yourself, and let's deal with this and get it over with asap."

The lawyer looked at her and smiled. "My wife and I have adopted one of your children. He has been such a blessing to our family. I realize this case is going to take a lot of work; however, I intend to do my work at no cost to you because I feel your organization contributes so much to our community and the health of children all over the world."

Rose replied, "I am so glad you are happy with our work; however, it is important to us we carry our own weight. We are privately funded and have the support from our benefactor to pay your bill. We believe and teach our children that we need to give and receive in fair trade. Therefore, to provide you with the most value, we will pay the bill. I have your retainer right here."

The lawyer replied, "I will begin right away. Could I come by and have a look at your center? I would like to get a better feel for what you do."

And with that, an appointment was set, and the fight was on.

Chapter 29

Although the staff tried to maintain a positive attitude toward their work and their life, the legal proceedings still put an edge on everything. Although they knew the welfare people would not be an issue, they still felt they needed to dial down a bit on their work. The problem everyone saw was that it may only be a short time for the adults, but it was a major stumbling block in the training in the young lives of these children... or was it?

***

All the children could feel the change in energy around the Matrix. The new children were more fragile as the change brought out their fears about being sent away, although they did not know any of the facts about the case.

The Windsurfers decided they needed to pitch in. The first thing was to stabilize the new ones, so they got them all together to have a chat with them and to help them focus on activities.

Goose decided he would take on leading this session, so he stepped up to the front of the group so they could see him. He then pointed to the backyard.

Once he had led them back to the cedars, they all sat down against the trees, hoping to do the same visualization as last time.

The visualization Goose led them in though, was supported by the trees, but, it focused on shifting the energy of the current situation.

"Start by focusing on your breath," he guided. "Once you feel you are in the zone, see a hole open in the top of your head. See the sun above. Let its energy flow down into the hole in your head so that its energy can flow down into your whole body, your whole being."

"See and feel it flowing down, filling your head. Relax. Let it flow down your neck and spread down into your arms and out the tips of your fingers. Feel it flow into and down your body through the chest, into the abdomen, and down your legs. Feel the energy flow out of your feet and down into the earth, connecting with Mother Earth."

He completed this visualization three times, then led them on "Now, bring the sun energy to the center of your body where your heart rests, then pull up the earth energy through your body to meet the sun energy at your core. Let the energies blend and let it flow out into your personal energy field. As you breathe, let the energy become more intense and larger, so it expands further and further.

Relax and enjoy the feeling of the power you have manifested, then expand the energy further, letting it reach out beyond this park and your tree friends. Let it stretch out to fill this city, this country, the entire planet, and the entire universe. Sit still for a moment and feel the power.

Now, bring the energy back into your mind and let yourself feel the energy of the people who are trying to stop us from being together. Breathe this feeling into their energy fields. See them release their attachments and become free. See them filled with universal love. See them happy and filled with love. Help them see themselves serving their highest purpose.

Now focus on the people involved in the trial, the judge, the lawyer, anyone else involved, filling them up with your loving energy.

Relax. Continue focusing on your breathing. Slowly, bring your consciousness back into your body and let yourself reconnect with your body and the outer world. When you are ready, take a deep breath, then open your eyes."

Not long after, everyone was sitting wide awake, beaming with loving energy. Once they were all back and ready, Goose got them up on their feet and started jumping around, yelling, and acting silly.

So much better than the sullen mood of not so long ago!

***

The very next day, the lawyer phoned Rose to announce that he was meeting with the Judge set for later that day. He felt strangely confident that things could be moved forward quickly. He knew this judge from previous cases; not one of his favorites, but today all was well.

Rose led the others in a centering visualization, then started the morning meeting to focus on how they would move forward for this day. She knew now that everything would be okay, too.

"We just have to trust the Universe that this is going to work out for everyone's best... including the people who have created this lesson!" she laughed. "We just have to have faith in the lawyer that he can bring this around to a successful conclusion in the shortest possible time.

I suggest for now that we all just carry on as usual, but make sure you keep yours, and everyone else's, energies high and positive."

With that, everyone headed off to do their usual duties.

Later in the afternoon, the lawyer did call back. He asked if he could stop over. He had something important to discuss.

Not very much later, everyone congregated in the boardroom with the lawyer.

"The judge has agreed with the petition to have the trial moved forward since it severely impacts the well-being of these children. He told me the claimants will try to drag out the time to frustrate the case, but he has ordered they provide a representative to meet with him before the end of the month. If they do not follow through on the order, they will be in contempt of court and the case will proceed without them.

Before I leave today, I would like to speak with the person who was on the boat."

Mike then looked at the lawyer and told him he would go get her and have her appear. (literally)

A couple of minutes later, Merle arrived. The lawyer thought nothing unusual about the fact that Mike did not accompany her. Merle introduced herself, then sat down at the table.

"How did you get the captain of the ship to change his course so that the boat docked here rather than following his planned route?

That is the critical point in the entire case," he said to her. "Did you threaten him or use any weapons?"

"I just smiled intently at him and politely suggested that he would do a lot of kids a big favor if he were to change course. I have a very persuasive smile." She laughed, then looked at the lawyer in the same way as she had looked at the captain.

He sat there; his mind completely blank for several minutes as Merle held his gaze.

He closed his eyes and took a deep breath, then said, "I see. Yes. You do have an amazing smile. Would you mind coming with me to meet the judge as soon as I can set up another appointment?"

Merle giggled under her breath, then concurred with the lawyer.

Several days later, Merle and the lawyer sat in front of the judge in his chambers. Before the judge could say anything at all, Merle smiled at him. He succumbed on the spot.

A couple more days later, the lawyer met again with the board at the Matrix.

He had a shocked look on his face as he told them, "I have never seen that judge act so fast. He told me, there is a law on the books that states that any case that can be shown to be not in the best interest of the people can be dismissed. Once dismissed, someone cannot re-open it for any reason.

The judge said that when he met Merle; he realized she was just an ordinary girl with a glorious smile. There was no possibility that any crime could have been committed. After all, the only reason she was on the boat was to get help for the pilot of her small boat, who had mysteriously fallen ill.

He has now forwarded the case to a council of judges for their concurrence. This is only a formality. I think we can say this trial has met its successful conclusion."

With that, everyone clapped and cheered.

The lawyer then added, "It would be my privilege to be your counsel in any situation if another need arises. I am also changing my career focus to be an advocate for child safety. I see the splendid work you have done and are doing. The children, including my own son, have benefited through your efforts. I want to be part of the healing. Thank you for being here."

And with that, he stood up, bowed, and made his way to the door.

***

And not to end this part of the Matrix saga at this point. About a week after the judge's counsel concurred with the judge, there was a knock on the boardroom door as the morning meeting began.

Mike opened the door and saw the three ladies from the government office standing there. The only difference (albeit a huge one!) was that they were all smiling. Mike invited them in.

Not wanting to interrupt their meeting, the lady who had been the representative for them in the prior meeting, spoke to the group "Good morning, sorry to interrupt, but it seemed to me that this was probably going to be the only time of day we knew you would all be together. We wanted to speak with you as a group about a couple of items if you don't mind." Then she smiled again.

Rose invited them in to sit, then offered them coffee and biscuits, but the spokes lady laughed, saying to her, "I really loved that tea we had last time. Could we have some more, please?"

They all laughed too, as Beth fetched them some Destiny Tea.

Once they were all together again, she began her prepared speech. She seemed a little nervous, as it was rare she found herself in such a personal situation with board members of a children's organization.

She began, "We collectively have never had the honor of witnessing or visiting such a fine organization as you people have created. What we have seen here astounded us.

When we heard you had retained a lawyer to assist you in eradicating this blight, we all went to see him to offer support. He then introduced us to the judge handling the case. In minutes, your case was resolved. We told the judge that your organization was the best thing that could ever happen to children, and if there was ever going to be a crime, it would be to allow these perpetrators to get their hands on these precious people."

She stopped speaking for a moment, so the board members could enjoy this praise, then continued, "After the council of judges had closed the case, clearing your organization from wrongdoing, the lawyer invited us back for a visit. If you open the door, I think you will find our new partner in our Children's Advocacy Group standing at the door."

Mike again opened the door, and sure enough, the lawyer was standing there with a big smile on his face. (There were a lot of big smiles on this day!)

She again spoke, "When we met again, we all realized that we were all fed up and frustrated with our jobs. When we first got these jobs, we believed we had become protectors of children but found ourselves protectors of ridiculous laws and bureaucratic power struggles. We all decided that enough was enough, so we handed in our resignations, and now here we are. Although independent of your organization, we offer our services and support to you in whatever way we can."

About a week later, there was an article in the local newspaper about the issue, and that the lawsuit was terminated.

The local citizens, especially the families who had adopted Matrix Children, were elated about the news, so they threw a big celebration for the victory.

Things only got better around this town as time moved on, however...

Chapter 30

Things at the Matrix returned to normal pretty quickly, although the Wind Surfers seemed more mature and very confident. Nobody really knew why, but the fact that they looked and felt great was really all that mattered.

Since things were going so well, Mike decided it was high time for a ride on his motorcycle. It had been a long time since he sat on that seat! Beth was too busy to take any time off, so he decided to take a few days to go for a ride on his own... or as on his own as he could get!

He set out early in the morning, looking forward to some steep and winding mountain roads. The twisting and turning, along with the amazing scenery, would be the best medicine for him.

When he stopped for lunch, he picked a nice place along a dirt road where he could sit under a huge tree. Of course, he chose a cedar tree! As he sat there quietly, Merle came forward.

She was not one to be meek about anything, however; she approached him rather quietly. Mike sat patiently, waiting for her to speak.

Then she said "Mike, I know you are doing this ride because you need to have some alone time but since your alone time always includes me... Would you teach me how to drive your motorcycle?"

Mike laughed and laughed. "This ought to be interesting! Should be good for practicing our integration too. Sure. Let's find somewhere suitable and give it a go. You have to promise me you will do as I ask, though, and not get too crazy!

He drove down the road for a while and soon found an abandoned parking lot. Fortunately, there was an old store with it that obviously had been closed for a long time. Mike parked the bike near the store and nipped around back.

A moment later, Merle walked around the corner and headed for his bike.

Mike laughed and said to her "Finally, you get to wear my clothes! And you can't kick me this time because you are on the outside!

Merle laughed and sat on the bike, feeling the beautiful beast under her.

She always was a pretty fast learner. Learning to ride a motorcycle brought her to a new level of connection with the body they shared. It was one thing walking or getting dressed or any other mundane activity, but she had few memories of anything similar to help her in getting used to balancing this beautiful machine as she learned to master it.

Mike set up some big rocks in a row separated enough for her to wind between them. It took a few tries, but she eventually made it through without stopping or spilling the bike. Mike cringed quietly each time she lost her balance but his lesson for the day was just to be patient... and quiet. After a few more hours of practicing, Merle could pass through the course at a pretty good speed, so the next lesson would be driving on the road. Before long, she was getting the hang of it. Mike really put her through the paces, and she handled every step like the pro she is with everything else.

Pretty soon Mike was riding on the back seat ... so to speak.

It happened that several of the staff were standing outside the Matrix when they arrived back a few days later. Everyone laughed and cheered when they saw the motorcycle coming toward them, but everyone stood absolutely aghast when Merle stepped off the bike.

She announced she was now officially a biker chick!

***

The members of the Wind Surfers were really excited to see Merle pull up on the motorcycle, not just because it was her driving the bike, but for their own reasons.

During the time Mike was away, the gang had held several meetings to decide how they wanted their future to unfold. Now that they had reached some decisions, they wanted to discuss them with Mike and Tomas. Before Mike had even gotten settled in, they had the room all set up with the chairs in their full circle (like the Knights of The Round Table!) along with drinks and appies on a side table.

It was Hummingbird that opened the discussion (He had really chosen an appropriate name because he could not sit still!) "We are glad you are back guys, but we are glad that we have had time to have discussions on our own with you gone. We want to run some stuff past you. Raven is going to lead the first discussion."

With that, Raven took a deep breath, then began, "We know that it was decided to keep us separated from the others here at the Matrix. We understand this is to protect us from uninformed eyes and we appreciate this, however, life has a way of keeping everything going and changing

With the situation we have just moved through as a perfect example, we each realized that we can only be of full service if we have the freedom to make such choices ourselves."

Raven paused for a minute, looking at Mike and Tomas, then continued, "The new group of members has had an extremely challenging time since they arrived because of circumstances well beyond their comprehension. We, as a group, decided that we were going to jump in and help them to not only survive this ordeal but to use it to move forward.

We understood that the court order prevented the staff from helping these people to begin their lessons, however; we are not staff, so the order did not apply to us. You know that old adage 'kids will be kids!' Well, we were!

The new children were looking very fearful. We thought they might pull too far into themselves, so we decided to take some action. They are all really settled in now and we are building relationships with them. Had we obeyed all these directives meant to protect us, things would be quite different here today.

We deeply appreciate that you support us in thinking for ourselves, and this, we believe, has been an opportunity to prove that we are mature enough to be responsible people.

We realize that once we mature into our full beings that we will need to take care not to expose our special natures in front of others as it could cause problems. We strongly feel that we need to just be open to the way our lives unfold and not have to feel that we need to be protected."

With that, he stopped and waited for discussion.

Mike and Tomas both sat quietly for a moment, not wanting to react to Raven's discourse emotionally, then Tomas looked at Mike, and then the gang, and replied, "We are so proud of you people. You have been through so much in your short lives and you have grown and matured far beyond our wildest expectations. We agree wholeheartedly with your decisions."

Tomas then looked at Mike, who offered, "It has always been our policy that the children would have the right to participate in whatever decisions needed to be made regarding their own personal growth, and even your own expression of life here at the Matrix. Kudos to you all for making this momentous decision."

Hummingbird then suggested they take a break, then reconvene in a few minutes when everyone was ready.

***

Now, since that hurdle was over with, Mike and Tomas could really see a change in the energies of the gang. They knew this second discussion was going to be even more interesting.

They could hardly wait to find out what surprises were in store for them now!

When everyone was back in their seats, it was Phoenix who had the lead in this next discussion. His smile was so big, he looked like he was going to explode if he did not get what he was going to say off his chest really quick!

"We have also been discussing some other matters that affect our futures collectively. We feel that now is the time for us to be creating a vision of what our futures will look like. We know we do not know what projects we will be asked to take part in, but we know that we will do, at least most of them, as a group," he started.

Just for emphasis, as hard as it was for him to pull it off, he sat quietly for as long as he could, then he continued "We have been discussing how we can be most effective in these future events and realized that it would be difficult for a group as large as ours to do covert work without being obvious."

Phoenix was barely containing himself, and with Hummingbird sitting beside him practically dancing on his chair, he could not hold on much longer, so he blurted out "We want to form a band!"

With that, all the gang jumped up and down laughing and making whooping sounds!

Mike and Tomas just sat there, completely stunned. It had not even occurred to them they were even conscious of their having a future that might have this kind of requirement. They stared at each other in amazed disbelief. Then they started laughing too, enjoying the kibbitzing going on around them.

When things calmed down again, Mike asked, "What kind of band do you see yourself being, Phoenix?"

"Well, we had quite a few discussions about this. We finally realized that we would need to travel light and quickly, so the musical instruments we play should fit our overall needs, so we have decided to become a chorale and flute band. Singing is our second nature, and the flutes will be easy to carry."

With that, everyone started jumping up and down again in excitement. Even Mike and Tomas joined right into the celebration.

So, they began making plans to create this band. They purchased various types of flutes. Mike suggested they hire a flute teacher, but the kids all laughed at him. Once the flutes arrived, they each picked one instrument and started playing it like they had been practicing for years.

Mike said to Tomas, "Isn't it amazing how people can just do things so easily if they are allowed to be cleared of their old belief systems. No arguing in the mind, just do it!

Mike said, "I remember in a book I read a long time ago where a guy was wandering in a hardware store with a fellow who was an earlier version of us. As the guy walked around the store, he heard what sounded like someone playing a really tinny guitar. When the fellow found out it was his friend, he said that he didn't know he played the guitar. His friend looked at him with a scornful look and told him, that anyone can do anything they want if they can just get their old beliefs out of the way. I think this rings true here, eh, guys!"

Soon there was wonderful music everywhere. It rang like piped music, but even better. Phoenix and Papi began collaborating on writing songs, while the others were choreographing some great stage presentations.

During a break one day, Papi pulled out a tin whistle and started playing some Irish lilts she heard in her head. Everyone in the room started dancing to the hypnotic music. When Papi had finished a song, Beth asked her where she found the tin whistle. In return, she got an eye that asked why anyone would ask such a silly question. Beth laughed, and Papi continued playing.

Only to outdo Papi, Goose walked in and began accompanying her with Uilleann Pipes-Irish bagpipes! This was going to be one entertaining group!

Now if we can just contain them so they don't give away all their secrets.

***

The music was an important step for everybody. Most importantly, it created an opportunity for the gang to really learn to work together. After all, great music is created when many individuals harmonize.

Music is also a feminine energy, as it is very nurturing. This would really help the boys to learn to balance their male and female aspects.

The boys had also created another situation that reinforced their female sides, that is, stepping in to take care of the new children.

All this feminine energy definitely had the effect that everyone was waiting for. The first one to transition was Goose. He woke up one morning and just felt that he could not get himself out of his bed. He said he felt like he was not in charge of his body, it just wanted to lie there. He asked Falcon to go get Mike or Tomas, so they could help him.

Both of them arrived soon after. They smiled when he told them how he felt. They smiled back too and congratulated him that he was the first of the Wind Surfers to begin the transition to full maturity. The reason he could not move his body was that during the night, his female aspect had been born. Mike and Tomas were looking at her!

Mike and Tomas instantly converted into Merle and Tarita, then sat on the side of the bed. Tarita started rubbing her arms and legs, trying to help her to wake up. It took a while, but eventually, Goose could move herself and sit up.

Merle cautioned her to take her time and offered her some water. It was another 10 minutes before she attempted to move again, and then suddenly she was up on her feet. The ladies gave her a big hug each and welcomed her, then just as quickly male Goose was back.

"I felt the whole thing," he laughed excitedly. "That was really neat. I heard you guys talking to me and felt you touch me, but it felt different. I am hungry though, so I asked her to come back in, so we could go eat."

***

Back in the boardroom, an emergency meeting was called, so that Merle and Tarita could discuss this morning's event with the others.

Merle led the conversation, saying, "Our first has arrived, so we need to be on high alert and prepared for the others. I bet that now that Goose has expressed, it will not be long before the others do."

"Anything you can suggest, Merle?" asked Beth.

"The resident staff need to be ready and aware of what to do. One of us needs to be available each night in case any of them has a problem transitioning. Best safe than sorry, even if we have invested a lot of training for this moment."

And Merle was absolutely right. Within a month, Papi had six new girlfriends! None had any serious issues in the transition, and they all expressed themselves in the same way as Goose.

Now they could get on with the big stuff!

Chapter 31

The most important focus at the Matrix was helping the boys become comfortable with their new identities. The transitioning processes integrating both parts of their new form required nothing short of miracles. How many other people have had to learn how to be both genders at the same time and still accept themselves?

Although the other children required ongoing attention, there was enough staff to keep them on the go, so that the key staff could direct their attention to this new and wonderful opportunity for a while.

The first exercise was to help them get used to seeing each other in female form. This was easier than when Mike and Tomas first met Merle and Tarita since they had been already conditioned to accept that they each would transition at some point, but that the entire group (except Papi) would do the same thing.

Rather than focusing on what had occurred, they decided that the morning rituals would be the best place to encourage acceptance, therefore it was business as usual, except that they would be isolated for the interim.

They all shared the issue of managing the transitioning. It kept happening without intention, so, as they were doing their morning yoga, each one of them would be male one moment and female the next. The transition was not gradual either. It was like a bubble popping, and then the other expression would be there.

It was several weeks before the boys learned to manage the shifting. In the meantime, yoga was hilarious!

Once they had finished playing yoga, the next part of the day's program was always visualization practice. Each of them sat having a two-way chat with themselves for weeks until it was natural. At first, the female aspects found it difficult to express themselves. However, with much patience, everything worked out, with one exception... Condor's female aspect could not verbalize at all.... but she came out signing like crazy!

As the gang settled into their new life, Mike and Tomas watched and helped, like a pair of mother hens. One day, Tomas said to Mike, "Have you noticed how different they look in their female forms from the way we look?"

"I noticed that, too. Merle and Tarita are distinctly unique characters from us. They look similar to us, but... different."

"This new version is sleeker. Their faces and body shapes are more similar, so when they transition, there is not so much visual difference. This will make them more efficient in their work, as they appear to be more integrated."

"It was absolutely brilliant that they all took on names that were not gender specific."

"Yes, this is going to be a real asset for them, not that we are any less amazing ourselves!" Tomas laughed as he felt a kick in his side (for old times' sake!)

***

The transitioning process was well under way, and the boys felt comfortable expressing themselves either way. It was time for them to introduce themselves to the other children.

The new group of children had been living in the Matrix for long enough now that they had experienced many novel events, and even had survived a few of their own. Seeing boys transition into girls right in front of them should not be a big deal, right?

The staff called a meeting to discuss how they were going to do this. Their concern was not about protecting them but ensuring that they had mentally prepared the new group for the introduction. As yet, there were so many things going on around them. They were not aware that Mike and Tomas were also Merle and Tarita. The icing on the cake would be if they knew Tarita and Papi were the butterflies they sometimes enjoyed, and now Papi and Goose were conjuring up musical instruments! Nothing abnormal here!

This was no place for fearful or closed-minded individuals! They would likely go screaming out of the building like crazy people if they were not ready.

The new children did not know why they were being assembled this day, but since nothing but good things had happened for them since they arrived, it must be another good thing that was about to happen.

Before they got too fidgety, they heard some really great music. The double door entryway flung open and in paraded 7 young ladies, each playing flutes!

And wasn't the music great! All the children jumped out of their seats and started dancing to the music and yelling sounds that just seemed to belong.

The staff members came in behind the musicians. They couldn't believe their eyes! It was like they were looking at a different group of children!

What was really great was that the children had not even noticed who the girls were. They just saw people playing music they loved.

They played and played and played, then Hummingbird submitted to his inner bird and began flipping and jumping high off the ground. Again, the new children thought this was so cool, so they started doing it too! Some of them could jump over twice their own height!

Things just kept getting crazier. The children were almost in ecstasy, so Rose suggested to Papi that they play some more mellow tunes to slow things down. Against their wishes, Papi and the girls complied. It was not long until they had fallen asleep in their chairs... the music had hypnotized them... Hmmm!

So much for the afternoon chat about the girls/boys!

The children sat still and relaxed in their chairs for a very long time. The music had opened the door to their dreamland. This created a great opportunity for some healthy programming.

Rachel appeared over the children. She had a special wand with her this day. She waved it over the children, causing sparkly dust to fill the room. It floated down right into their faces, then they breathed it in.

They each took a deep breath, then... They looked like balloons losing their air. Their faces, which usually looked protective and distant (when not listening to good music!) now looked very serene. Their taut bodies, ready to jump up and escape, became relaxed and passive.

As they relaxed and took more deep breaths, a very noticeable smelly odor became very evident. Every time they took a deep breath, the odor became more intense. What an awful smell! A skunk would be jealous!

Rachel continued to monitor each child. Then, when she felt it was time, she waved her wand again. The offensive odor vanished!

For a third time, she waved her wand. The children woke from their dreams. Rachel smiled at her people, then disappeared.

The children stretched and moved around, trying to come back to life. Some of them were hungry, so Rose called the cafeteria and had drinks and goodies sent over. These children deserved a delightful treat after the amazing work they had just done.

The world these children had come from had just become a foggy, distant memory that meant nothing to them anymore.

***

From that day forward, the training was so easy for them. They were like people lost in the desert thirsting for water. They just could not get enough.

It soon became time to assess the children to determine which species each of them was. Each group seemed to have less apparent issues to tell whether they were Homo Sapiens or Homo integratis. Only time would tell.

These children comprised an older age group compared to the first two. This meant there was less time to prepare them for transition if they were Homo integratis. The plan then was to treat them all as if they were. After all, the training was more about respecting and empowering both the female and male aspects of each individual...

Well, except for Tarita and Papillon. Who knows what spectacular events await them!

Chapter 32

Tarita received the message that it was time to create a project to let Papi test out her new wings. Papi had put everything, including her heart, into clearing herself. She was learning to power her butterfly with Divine Love, and now she felt she was ready to soar.

Tarita decided that whatever project they should do might as well be close by in case there was a problem. She thought and thought about what they might do. She brought the question to the morning council meeting.

"I need to give Papi a big job so we can test her level of working in the Power. I have been mulling it over in my head but could not come up with anything. I want to keep the project close to home here just in case I need some help."

They all sat pondering the situation over for a few minutes, then Mike said "I know! It's a good thing that Beth and I are so familiar with this area. Orphanages!"

"Great idea, Mike. There are at least two of them in this city. Maybe seniors care facilities too. I am sure they would enjoy a visit from a butterfly, especially a Golden Butterfly!"

Tarita smiled and said, "Those are just perfect! Now that we have answered that question, can we come up with a task for her? I would like her to do more than just fly there and be a pretty butterfly for the entertainment of the children or older folks."

They discussed the situation for quite a long time. By the time the meeting wrapped up, Tarita had a good plan for testing Papi. She had every confidence in the young girl. Ever since she had gone into that deep sleep, she had become more than an exceptional student.

***

Tarita had really put Papi through the gauntlet. She knew the potential inside this girl, but she also knew that independent side that wanted to do things her way. If she were to become the great butterfly she could be, she needed to learn to carry out directives as she was given. Papi needed to learn the difference between self-thinking and working as an open vessel with the Universe!

Papi had taken on looking after the garden once she felt better again. She felt bad for hurting her plant friends. (Luckily, they understood and had forgiven her). The plants just loved her, and for her, they grew tall and strong with flowers one could smell almost from the buildings, while the vegetables tasted so good, they made one's mouth water from the fragrances of cooking them.

She, like Mike, was now a consummate conversationalist with her plants. Encouraging them to grow and be healthy was one of her favorite pastimes. She projected loving energy to them by sitting with them and envisioning them soaking in Universal light from the Cosmic. What more could our plant friends ever want?

Tarita realized this would be the tool for Papi's first mission then. She sat with Papi in the garden and chatted with her about her idea.

"I think this is going to be fun to do. I would like to fly to one of the local orphanages and see if I can inspire the children to become their best. Maybe I can help them just like I get to help my plant friends!"

Papi was so excited about the project, she became her butterfly on the spot. She was just about to fly off when Tarita stopped her and asked her to come back to her girl form.

"Remember, young lady, what we have been teaching you about discipline? You mustn't take off into these projects before we have agreed that we understand and agree about what you are about to do."

Papi sat down beside Tarita in the garden again and waited. She knew better than to pout, so she began working with the energy on her plant friends again.

"I know this is hard for you, Papi, but in time, you will understand the importance of what we are teaching you. We must work in harmony together. It can make the difference between a project working out and it becoming a failure. Lives may be at stake if you do not learn this lesson. I can tell you are still resisting this lesson. We need you to work your way through this one."

"Now, I want you to go play with the new children for a while. I will let you know when you can go on your assignment." With a big hug, Papi wandered off to find the other children.

Once Papi was out of sight of Tarita, she immediately transitioned to butterfly. Papi knew better. This job was an easy decision for a butterfly like her... and she was going to show Tarita she did not need to be treated like a young child.

Having already found an orphanage nearby, she could easily fly there, check it out, and fly back within an hour, so off she went.

She was right. The orphanage was right where she had thought. She flew around the building looking for anyone, but mostly for the children. As she flew to the back of the building, she found them outside, playing.

What she failed to notice was that a young boy had a butterfly net. He was chasing anything he could see that flew.

Papi heard the young boy yell in excitement... too late.

***

Page 312

Papi flew right into the net at full speed (for a butterfly). It knocked her unconscious right on the spot.

The young boy grabbed her and ran inside to his room, where he had prepared a glass jar to put her in. It is a good thing he was smart enough to punch holes in the lids so she could breathe!

Looking around through groggy eyes, Papi realized she was a prisoner. Butterfly tears streamed down her tiny little cheeks. What was this disobedient butterfly to do now?

***

Tarita sauntered back into the Matrix, feeling somewhat apprehensive after her chat with Papi. She thought to herself, "That girl is a real test. She is so determined to do things her own way. I do hope she listened to me."

Many of the children were inside playing and dancing to music. She looked around to see if she could see Papi. No Papi!

She did not feel good about this. Hurrying throughout the entire building, trying in desperation to find this imp. No luck! She even checked her bedroom. Nope!

Papi was nowhere to be found! Her feelings had been right!

How to find her? She sat down in the break room. She focused on her breath until she reached the right place in her mind. Then, she reached out into the Universe looking for Papi's energy.

It only took a minute to find her. Once she connected with her energy, she could feel Papi crying. She then pulled Papi's consciousness into hers so she could see what Papi could see. The shock almost brought her back to the outside world!

She could see something clear wrapped loosely around Papi. Papi's energy felt fuzzy like she was not feeling well. She called into Papi's mind and asked her where she was. Papi could not remember. This was a disaster!

Tarita rushed back to consciousness and ran to find someone to tell them what had happened. Beth was walking by in the hall, so she grabbed her by the arm and pulled her to the couch. Tarita explained what had happened.

"What are you going to do, Tarita?"

"I can feel her energy, but I can't get a fix on where she is, so I am thinking I will track her down by following her energy. Let the others know so we can all be ready to help if need be. Do you have time to do a connection with me, so you can stay in touch as this unfolds?"

"I was going to meet Mike for coffee. Let me just run and let him know, then I will do so. We need to get that girl back and fixed, once and for all!"

***

It did not take Tarita long to find Papi. The orphanage was only a few blocks away. She started searching for the girl (or butterfly, in this case). Listening through the Universal web, she heard Papi sobbing.

The boy had put her in a jar and was carrying her around, showing off his great catch. The children were all too busy ogling Papi to notice a second golden butterfly in their midst.

For now, there was nothing Tarita could do. She needed the boy to put the jar away so there were no lookie-loos nearby to see how she was going to help Papi get out of her prison.

Tarita flew up to the ceiling in his room, where no one could see her. She landed just at the right place where no one could see her, but she could easily watch the children below.

It took a while, but finally, the children lost interest in the golden butterfly, so the boy took the jar back to his room and placed it on a windowsill.

"Perfect, now to get her out of there." She flew up to the jar, landing on it. Papi could see her right away but seemed to not react to Tarita appearing.

Tarita called to Beth... She then asked her to call everyone to send energy to Papi. Soon, the healing energy flowed, helping her feel better. Her mind became clearer, and finally, she recognized Tarita and called out to her.

"Think yourself out of the jar, Papi. You have to do it yourself. See yourself free and flying home!"

After a few seconds, Papi took a deep butterfly breath and found herself on her way home. She knew she was in big trouble!

Chapter 33

As Papi slept that night, snuggled into her own little bed, she dreamed. It was not a dream she ever wanted to dream, but she knew she had caused it. As she slept, she saw her beautiful butterfly wings fall off her back. They fell to the ground.

All that was left was a little girl, no longer special, just a little girl.

She woke after the dream, crying as she had never cried before. Once she was awake, she decided she was going to try to turn into her butterfly, just to prove the dream was just a dream... It was not.

Papi climbed back into bed and cried herself to sleep. In the morning, she stayed in bed, trying to pretend that the morning had not come. When Beth came in to check on her, she pretended she was still asleep, but Beth kept rocking her from side to side. When that didn't work, Beth resorted to something she knew would work. She knew butterflies were always ticklish!

Papi opened her eyes and glared at Beth. She did not want to get out of bed this morning. Papi knew

she was going to hear about what she had done...
and she did not want to hear it!

Knowing Beth would not leave her alone until
she got out of bed, she climbed out. Beth did not even
give her a chance to get dressed but sent her down to
breakfast in her pajamas. There was going to be no
sneaking back to bed, and no hanging about. The day
was underway even if it had to be done in night
clothes.

The other children giggled when Papi entered
the cafeteria wearing her pajamas. She knew better
than to cause a ruckus, especially today.

After breakfast, Papi rushed up to her room to
get dressed and prepared for the day. She was not
going to stand out for everyone to laugh at. No siree!

When she came back to the yoga room, Tarita
was waiting for her. She took Papi aside, asking her
how she was feeling.

Papi quietly replied in her tiny little voice, telling
her about the dream and her subsequent failed
attempt at becoming her butterfly.

"Because of your choice to disobey me, your
wings have been removed for the time being, Papi.

You need to understand that having the ability to become a butterfly at will is a special gift from the Universe.

The instructions I gave you were not from me. I did not mean for them to control you. They gave you the opportunity to submit and push past your ego. You must learn that if you are going to work as one of us, with the gifts you have received through Universal energy, you have to submit completely to Universal Love. You cannot be a true servant of God if your ego is in the way."

Tarita stopped speaking for a few moments to allow Papi to absorb what she had told her, then she continued.

"We have taught you how to move into the energy of Universal Love. We have taught you how to move the Kundalini energy, so you can connect with Source. After break this morning, you will meet me, and we will begin again. We will do these exercises until you get it right. You have a wonderful, special skill the Universe has bestowed upon you, Papi. You will not have your wings again until you submit and accept to working your skill through love."

"How will I know I have learned how to submit, Tarita?"

"At some time in the future, an opportunity will arise for you to act in a selfless way. If you choose to complete this task, they will return your wings. Until then, you are just a wonderful little girl."

Papi felt like they had thoroughly punished her for what she did. She was not happy with her punishment, but deep down inside, she knew Tarita was right. She headed off to yoga, and for the rest of her day.

At break time, Rose approached her, offering her a warm cup of tea. Papi drank it. She loved hot teas.

Soon she found herself alone out in the backyard, down by the garden. She leaned against her favorite cedar tree to relax. It was not long before the tea worked its magic.

Papi closed her eyes. It was like she was in a dream; a dream that felt like flying, only fast. Soon, she faced a beautiful, young, but mature lady who looked like her. This woman took Papi's hand, then turned her around, pointing far away. Papi stood staring at her future life... as if it were in the past.

Papi then knew what her future destiny was. It was a destiny she truly wanted. She knew then that she had to learn to listen to the elders and to do as they bade her do.

***

The next morning, Rose called all the gang into the break room. She told them she had a special treat for them. Once they had settled in, she led them into the deep recesses of their minds through a special visualization.

It was then that the special treat occurred. Rachel, ever elegant in a shimmering violet gown, smiled radiantly before them. Until now, Papi was the only one of these children who had interacted individually with Rachel, but they all knew it was a very special occasion, so they were in awe when she appeared.

"*I am Rachel. I serve the Universal God that created this earth and all that exists. I invite you to join me in this moment of knowing yourself through* the eyes of God," she said, as she looked directly at each member of the gang.

"It gives me great pleasure to speak with you on this day. Now that you are becoming mature individuals, it is time for you to know yourself as I know you. I am pleased with how well each of you has done with adapting to your new form.

It also pleases me you have integrated yourselves into such wonderful beings. You are the first of your kind to express in this high level of evolution. You will now each begin to learn the lessons that will support you in living out your highest destinies.

Remember, it is always your choice whether you attain your highest purpose. You must let your ego go. It has no place in our work." As she said this, she smiled at Papi.

"Your purpose as human beings, no matter which species you are a member, is to grow as an individual, for as you grow, the Universe grows. Mankind was given the breath of life for the sole pleasure of the Cosmic.

Your purpose, no matter how evolved you are, is to embrace who you are at that level, and to strive to become all that you can be, until selflessly and completely you reunite with the Cosmic by vibrating at the same frequency.

This will take not only a great deal of work to attain these highest levels, but it will also take willingness. Willingness to let go of the illusion of control as espoused by the ego itself.

The ego, in human beings, only serves two purposes. First, so you recall each day who you have manifested into in this lifetime, and second, to protect you. You learn this protection through the lessons provided to you as a youngster.

You must now endeavor to accept that you were born safe, by your very nature. The protection provided by your ego, in fact, makes you more unsafe, so it is in your best interest to let it go, and let it serve in its proper service only.

It is by surrendering the ego that you can know heaven. It is also by committing to a life driven by the ego that you will know hell. They are not places in the

Universe. They are reflections of how you live your life, in the here and now."

With this, Rachel concluded and faded away. Her amazing smile, being the last vision of her presence with the children.

Chapter 34

The man was mad! Spitting nails mad! He did not like it one bit that his business was being messed with. Something had to be done about this situation. Gritting his teeth as his stomach churned acid up his throat, he obsessed. He needed an answer now, or he would not be having a business left!

Twice, now three times, someone had stolen his merchandise, right from under the nose of the people he most trusted. The worst part was that he couldn't seem to find any of them. They had just disappeared!

"First, the children with the gang at that port city. I have worked with these guys so many times with no problem, and now I cannot even find a trace of them!"

He scowled at himself. "That second bunch, I had them so secure, no one could have gotten to them. And then that virus hit and ruined everything... and then those citizens fired their perfectly good government and took over the country! What gives them the right?

And the third ones! I had them on a boat. How much safer can it be... then the stupid captain decided to change course. Change course all right... if I ever catch him.

Now those guys who bought the children are threatening me because they didn't receive their merchandise! It's not my fault!"

After he took some medication for his high blood pressure (in the form of strong alcohol), he thought about the three situations without going back into his tantrum.

"There must be some similarities with each of these three situations. I need to find out whether there are any links. Let's see what I can figure out."

He scoured over all the information he had collected. These operations were carried off so covertly there were never many articles about them in any newspapers.

The first situation left him completely blank. There just was no information to be found. He never did find that motorcycle gang that supposedly had everything tied up in that area! What could have happened to those guys?

The second situation was not much better. The people he had bribed to hold the children were now in a special prison. They would never know freedom again.

He tried to find information about the agency that had interceded to help rid the country of that virus. All he found out was that they had taken the children from his prison and back to the country where they were based. No one seemed to know where the children had gone from there.

He could not fathom how thirty children could just disappear. They had to have been moved somewhere, someway, by someone. Who had the answers?

The third situation seemed to provide more clues than the others, but still not enough to give him the answers he needed. Apparently, there was a woman, or was it a man?

According to his sources, this person got onto the island where he had faked holding the children, but no one knew who they were or where they went.

The people he had spoken with said a woman had shown up to sniff around, while others said it was a man. Then someone said they saw the woman hire a boat so she could get off the island. No one knows where the man went. No one has seen him since.

"Then a woman shows up on the boat that we hired to haul these brats to the buyers. And for some unknown reason, the captain decided he should change course. I wonder if this woman is the same person!

How do I find out? And where did that boat and captain go? They just seem to have disappeared right off the earth."

**

Mike was glad to dive into some sleuthing. It had been so long since he had used his talents to solve a case. He looked forward to stretching those detective muscles again!

The adrenaline flowed as his inner investigator fought to find out who this person was. His sense was that it was one person or group that had perpetrated all three cases.

Merle had been monitoring her target for quite a while, to keep up on his activities. Even with that, he never divulged his identity or if he worked with a group or alone. That would have made things so much easier!

Even with all his skills, he had no luck in finding anything about him. He even went through his people at the police station to contact Interpol. They came up blank.

The people at Interpol knew about the occurrences but had come up with nothing tangible. There were bits of information, but it was not of enough value to nail anything down.

They said they had several people around the world with their ears to the ground. They would let them know if they found anything.

"If only I had something to draw," he muttered to himself. "I need to connect with his energy. I need to find something... or someone who has a clue for me."

Then the light went on! How obvious! They had processed all the children through his system. He may not have ever interacted with any of the children, but surely the people who guarded these children must have referred to who they were working for at least once!

Mike called a meeting. He told them what he had realized, and how they needed to interview each of the children. There must be someone who could provide some clues.

"I think that if we select children who have already developed a strong sense of self to ask, they might feel comfortable enough to dig back into those memories. Wouldn't our best bet our gang of seven?" Beth offered.

Mike agreed. "Yes, let's just see what we can find out from them."

Then Tarita said, "Maybe we can do a regression visualization to take them back to that time. That way we can get the information and do any healing that is necessary at the same time."

Rose then suggested, "I agree, but I think we should do this one person at a time, so we make sure we can focus on that person and ensure we get all the information we need safely.

In fact, how about videoing each session so we can review it if necessary? This person has avoided being noticed so far, even by Interpol. We will need every bit of information we can get!"

***

"I think I am going to start by finding that darned captain and his boat. He has to be somewhere. That boat can't just disappear into the air.

I know where the boat was registered, so that is the place to start. I know where the boat was last seen as well. What I do not know is what happened to the boat or the captain after they stole the children at that port."

***

Mike left ladies to handle the interviews, so he could do his own investigating. If he could find the captain of that boat, maybe he could discover who had hired him. Something about that island did not jive. Mike thought that it may have just been a rouse.

He was pretty sure he could find some valuable information when he went to interview the Port Authority officers.

His first stop after he arrived, out of courtesy, was the local police station. When he introduced himself, they all gave him a look of recognition. All that good work had really paid off! That made their cooperation much easier.

The duty police sergeant gave him the name of the officer in charge at the Port Authority, who could give him what information was on file. He said he would call him, let him know he was coming.

Upon arriving at the dock, Mike went straight into the Port Authority office, where the officer was waiting for him.

"The boat is still sitting here, Mike. After we apprehended the children, the captain of the ship abandoned it. It sat there for months until we finally impounded it. It is still in our storage compound."

"Great! Is it possible I can get access to it?" Mike asked. "In fact, maybe I can get someone from the police department to do some fingerprinting since we don't even know who this guy is."

"Good idea," he replied. "We would like to find out something about the boat so we can get it out of here. I am amazed that a boat can operate anywhere in this world while having no registration papers."

He later spoke with both the Port Authority officer and the Police sergeant.

"He wiped the boat absolutely clean. There was not even a hair to be found. There is just nothing to go on."

The Port Authority officer offered, "Yes, we checked into the name of the boat, and even it is bogus."

They all went silent for a moment, thinking about the situation, then Mike said, "I would like to have one more look. There must be a plaque on the boat somewhere that tells where the boat was built. If we can find it, at least we have a starting point."

Now building a history for it would be easy. The first step would be to reach out to the marine traffic division of the international coast guard. They should be able to give them some information.

It took Mike aback when the person at the registration office, almost by chance, told him he was the second person to enquire about this particular ship in recent days!

He was told they gave the other person no information because they refused to apply in writing. He then told Mike that if he would like to apply

following protocol, they would be happy to help him
out.

That done, Mike now had two valuable pieces
of information.

***

"These government bureaucracies! They
always want their pound of paperwork! Well, I don't do
paperwork! I guess I will have to travel there and see
if I can bribe someone to give me the information."

He was used to getting his own way. Money
was no object for him and there usually was at least
one hungry government employee willing to do a little
extra work to help his own bank account.

Reaching out through his network, he found his
employee. His search could begin.

Little did he know, the authorities were
expecting him, so they were ready. Unfortunately for
the man, they had recorded the whole payoff on a
security camera.

***

Now Mike had a picture of the person
suspected of the kidnappings. The police had no

information about this person yet. However, it would not be long.

Mike, on the other hand, needed nothing else. Once he had found a target, he could go to work. With a finished photo, all he, or more correctly Merle, had to do was to connect with his energy. Soon they would have all they needed. With his picture in hand, Merle knew it was indeed the man that she had been mind reading!

With the information he needed, he called the local Interpol agency to set up a meeting.

***

They met a couple of days later. The Interpol guys did not know about Mike's skills, so they were resistant to accepting how he found out who this guy was so quickly when they could not.

Mike smiled at them as he picked up his cell phone, calling his former Chief Detective. That took care of that! Now let's get down to business!

Mike started the conversation quickly, not wanting to give the officers the chance to continue trying to interview him. After all, he was not the criminal here.

"Now that you know who this man is, I am asking you to maintain surveillance on him only until I give you the word. The reason is that I need to find out if he has any more children stowed away somewhere."

"I think we can handle it from here," one officer replied. "This is police business now, not yours, even if you are some kind of wonder boy."

Mike figured he was trying to rattle him, so he paused for a moment, focusing his thoughts. Then he projected a great golden cloud into the room. In a flash, the local director of the Interpol Agency barged into the room.

He stared at his officers. "Why are you trying to intimidate this man? Do you not know who he is? If he wants us to maintain surveillance, then that is what we are going to do. There is still a lot of evidence to collect and prove up yet before we have a case. Without the information Mike has provided, you guys would still be nowhere."

Mike still had a lot of information to find out, as well. Hopefully, this guy wouldn't be any wiser too soon, at least not until he discovers the information the Port Officer gave him was the registration for a different boat.

Merle sensed that someone, maybe this guy, had kidnapped another group of children and was holding them hostage... somewhere.

Now, at least, he had a face. He had, sorry, Merle had easily extracted his identity. Now they needed to get to work to find out where the children were.

***

The man had connections everywhere. Getting information about the boat once he got his hands on the registration papers would be a cinch. One of his people was a computer hacker who owed him a huge favor.

The computer hacker did a quick search on a restricted website that kept information about where all the boats in the world were at this moment. He typed in the registration number and received the information on said boat.

He called the man, saying, "I have your boat, but I have bad news for you. The boat sank out in the Atlantic. It is sitting on the bottom."

"You are absolutely sure?" he demanded.
"That guy would go to any length to get away with
what he did! I will find him!" And with that, he
slammed the phone down.

The hacker closed the program and walked
away, not noticing the date of the sinking. It sank
twenty years before the right boat had docked with
the children!

***

Mike still needed more information about this
man. He headed back to the Matrix to find out what
the ladies had discovered. Rose gave him a dossier
filled with news about this man's activities.

His (Merle's) next step was to read his mind to
get any current information. She was especially
wanting any news to do with the new kidnappings.
Tarita sat nearby with pen and paper ready to copy
down anything Merle spoke. Rose had also set up the
video camera so they could review the information
after.

There was so much information to extract from
this man's mind. He had been a busy boy for a long
time.

She sifted through his mind. It was like searching for a missing piece of jewelry at the bottom of a sewer outlet. She garnered information about several of his past activities, which would be great for the police, but what she wanted were the plans for any new kidnappings.

This was a new process for her. Collecting data from someone's mind about past events was simple enough. It was already sitting there in a block of information. However, thoughts about a new project are often very nebulous, or loosey-goosey, in layman's terms. There could be variables not even thought of yet.

This made sorting through the chaff much harder. In fact, Merle found it very tiring, so it took several days and several more attempts to extract any useful information. But we know Merle, never hear this one saying, "I can't!"

She had to figure out how to access the information, then separate it from useless stuff. This man's mind was crowded with a lot of fuzzy information, but she did it!

Now they could move on to the next step-verifying the information she had attained. This was Mike's job.

The first step was to confer with the Interpol agents. By now, they were much more receptive to Mike and his skills.

The amount and the quality of information he provided astounded them.

Some of the information was the same as they had already collected. Seeing it come from another source increased the value of both collections.

One of the most important pieces of information Merle had found was where his home base was. Although he lived in various locations, he had a home base. They dispatched officers to each of the locations and told them to observe only.

They were a long way from arresting him, but they would only wait for so long... and as long as there was bona fide reason. It would not take long to build a strong case against him once they proved up the information they now possessed, but they realized the importance of completing the rescue of the next set of children.

The Interpol supervisors were pleased to leave the rescuing to Mike and his people. They did not have the resources to develop, manage, or complete a mission requiring the accessing, managing, and relocating of a large group of children.

***

That night, Merle had a dream. She saw an island, a little island, sitting off the shore in a remote area. She sensed the children, but could not see them. Maybe they were not there yet. She also sensed many dogs.

Chapter 35

Beth and Sheila had been very busy working with Tarita to help the Wind Surfers, as they loved to be called, in moving forward in their lives. The process they designed to cultivate the information about the man had worked far better than they had hoped. Now they had two projects to work on.

The first, of course, was the continuing development of the Wind Surfers. They needed to get them to a point where they could clarify and implement the tools they would need for their future projects. Since they were such an enthusiastic group, they always met the reception of extra activities and tools with great thirst.

The second project was more long-term. However, the best time to start a new project is right now. This was important to the longevity of the Matrix and any offspring.

The aim now was to find replacements for the man as a resource. Once the law apprehended him, that door would be closed. It would be easy to just become an orphanage and play the system, waiting for one child at a time, but the Matrix system needed specific large groups of children. Children who had been traumatized by wars or environmental catastrophes. These children could access the deeper resources of their souls once they had healed the trauma of their childhood events. Regular children just could not dig that deep.

This man, unknowingly, had been a great resource to the Matrix, and would continue to do so for the short term, but his time was now limited. New resources had to be discovered. The question was how to find these new resources.

Now that Mike had Interpol on his side, they would be helpful. However, being a huge worldwide bureaucracy with more work than they have resources for, the likelihood of them being a beneficial resource was minimal. There would need to be another.

How had they found the first group? And the second and the third? That was the place to start. Maybe they could access that technique to find more. There had to be more people on this planet who ran similar operations.

The first step would be to have a discussion with Rose since she had been the center point of this operation from even before the Matrix existed.

***

Rose was sitting in her office when the group came in. They all sat down at the counsel table and waited for her to join them as she always did. When they told her what they wished to discuss, Rose looked a little hesitant. She knew now that the time had come for her to confess.

"I feel I need to preface this conversation by saying that you each must develop your own strategy that allows you to find other child kidnapping operations. This ability will require an even higher level of Cosmic Communication.

The Cosmic has given us this access point as a starter. Remember, it is not just about the children. It is also about your own personal and spiritual development and fulfilling your own life purpose. If I continually fed you the information about these nefarious operations, you would have lost the opportunity to grow in a manner that is essential to your ability to achieve greater successes in the future."

She stopped speaking for a few moments to allow the information to soak in, then Mike spoke up and said, "Am I presuming correctly by your statements, that you have had previous interactions with Rachel than the ones we know about, maybe even before the very first day I met her, Rose?"

Rose composed herself, then waved her arm, and in a flash... Rachel sat in her place.

***

They all sat, stunned. The minutes ticked by. Not one of them moved. Finally, life flowed into their faces again.

"*I have left so many indications, telling you who Rose really is, but none of you caught them. Souls who vibrate at Angel level are quite capable of manifesting physical beings that operate almost independently from the Mother soul. Rose is an aspect of my soul, as are others I have found necessary to manifest from time to time.*"

She waited for a minute, then continued. "*Now that you know the truth about Rose, she will not return to continue working with you. Despair not, as it was planned that her position would become redundant. It is now time for Bethany and Sheila to become the driving force at the Matrix.*

Michael and Thomas will continue searching. There are so many children to find and bring home.

As always, I am here nearby in your time of need."

And with that, Rachel and Rose disappeared.

***

A new day began... and a new Matrix. Rose had been such a vital driving force to the operation... and now she was gone.

Once the shock had worn off, Beth and Sheila assessed the overall situation. They needed to get a clearer picture of the work and energy that Rose had provided so they could break it into jobs for them to take on. It was not all that difficult for Beth and Sheila to do this because, over the last few months, Rose had been assigning more and more duties to them. Now, they just had to take ownership of them.

"It is a very different sense of duty to the jobs when we know we are responsible for their whole outcomes instead of just doing our part, isn't it, Beth," Sheila said to her a few days later.

"It sure is, and I am glad that she had already immersed us in all the jobs ahead of time. Now, all we have to do is take charge of the paperwork and deciding who is going to do what. It is a good thing we have such a great team!" Beth replied.

***

Mike and Tomas met together the next day in the break room. The gang was off enjoying some free time, so this was a perfect time to sit and discuss how they were going to move forward from where they stood at present.

"I have something I would like to discuss with you before we do anything new," Tomas said.

Mike smiled and opened his hand to him, inviting him to continue. At that, Tomas spoke "We have each developed a good rapport with our female aspects. Tarita and I have regular and ongoing conversations to decide how we are going to handle any situation we become involved in. I suspect that you and Merle do as well. There is one thing we have not started doing, and I feel it is now time for us to move to that next level."

Mike looked at Tomas, not sure what he was implying, so Tomas continued, "We need to be able to have conferences freely with the four of us at one time. It is different for us than the Wind Surfers. They are so integrated that their male and female aspects automatically work in harmony. Being the older models, we are not born with that capacity. We, therefore, have to come up with a way to ensure that the four of us can freely discuss matters as separate individuals."

"Well, Tomas, everything else we have felt the need to do, we have accomplished. How do you propose to do this?"

Quick as a wink, both males transitioned into their female aspects. Merle smiled at Tarita, then laughed. "Boy, that Mike can sure be slow sometimes!"

For the first time, Merle felt a kick from the inside!

Both Tarita and Merle turned to each other on the couch and reached out their hands to each other.

They then closed their eyes, breathing together, while envisioning a room inside their minds. Soon, they had generated enough energy into the vision that it had become like a real physical room. It even had two couches to sit on!

Once the visualization had generated the desired result, they all sat together, separately. Having had the practice at the fishing cabin helped them in their efforts to communicate together, but now they were getting into the heavy stuff! They could now, in this room, each be individuals.

Merle laughed again "Nothing is difficult when you set your mind to it, is it Tarita?"

"Now let's get down to business. This is great, ladies. I can get to see again what I look like as a girl, Merle." Mike laughed as Merle kicked his leg, just for fun.

"This is a dynamite tool. I wonder if we need to be touching each other to do this or can we do it when we are apart? It would be great if we can do these get-togethers for some brainstorming when we are working on a project together, but not in the same location."

"Let's practice this format for now, and when we get comfortable with it, we can figure out how to move it up a notch. I love all these neat tricks we come up with," laughed Merle.

"Right now, since we are all here, let's talk about the Wind Surfers. They have come along so far since they first arrived at the Matrix. We need to keep instilling more training in them, so they have every advantage."

As Mike said that, there was a shuffle behind him. Tarita, who was sitting beside Tomas and opposite Mike and Merle, jumped in shock, then began laughing so hard she fell on the floor. Mike and Merle jumped up to look at what had made the noise behind them, only to see the six boys moving a long couch into place inside their mind room!

After they all had gotten back into a calmer presence, they rearranged the furniture so that the boys were sitting with them, forming a "U".

Mike again laughed and said, "Who is teaching who here? How did you guys know to do that?"

Goose looked at Mike with a look of something like a cat who caught that pesky mouse and said, "We were waiting for you guys to figure this out. We have been waiting for you to catch up for quite a while."

He then continued, "Now that you guys have caught up (the boys all laughed again), we feel there is something that needs to be attended to right away. You notice that someone is missing?"

It was then that the four of them realized Papi was not there.

Phoenix then continued the conversation. "We understand her wings got clipped after she misbehaved again. More important, Papi now understands the error in her choices. We also understand that she has to do something selfless, so she gets her wings back. We feel it is time for that to happen, as our group just feels so incomplete without her."

As Phoenix finished his statement, there was another noise, this time a whoosh, and there stood Rachel. She looked at the group, then said, "*I like this meeting room much better! It feels more natural to me!*"

Everyone laughed. They had rarely known Rachel to make a joke before. She was always so serious!

Rachel continued. *"Even angels have a sense of humor, you know!"*

She laughed again and continued. *"Yes, Papi has come a long way, and it is time for her to find out what she is made of. She will have her chance to prove herself soon. We all dearly miss our spiteful, but wonderful little butterfly!"*

***

Papi came into the room hoping to find the boys doing something interesting, but when she walked in, she found them doing a visualization process.

"Must be something serious they are doing," she thought to herself. "They look different from how they usually look when doing these quiet times. Guess I better find something else to do, so I don't bother them."

And with that, she headed out to the back for an enjoyable walk in the woods. That would be the next best thing to hanging out with her buds. It was okay with her that she was not taking part in whatever they were doing. It was part of the price for her disobedience. She knew that in time she would get to show the Cosmic that she had learned and accepted the importance of being part of the team by doing what she was asked, rather than running off and doing things her own way.

Papi so wanted her wings back! Being a normal little girl just was not what she wanted. After all, why would one want to be a cute little girl, when they can be a golden butterfly!

Papi headed out the back door, walking straight toward the garden. She thought maybe a friendly visit with the cedar trees and the plants in the garden would be a great way to while away the hours until the boys were back. She dreamed about playing music, laughing, and singing, and maybe even conjuring up some new musical instruments. That is so much fun!

The trees shook their branches in excitement at seeing their little Papi. They spread their boughs wide as she entered the cedar grove just so they could take in her vibrant energy. It looked like they were all giving her a big hug!

She had a favorite place to sit when she visited the trees, so as soon as she sat down, she flowed into the cedar tree energy. Papi felt so strong and so connected with the earth and the sky as she became one with the cedar energy.

She took a deep breath and let out an enormous sigh. As she released the air, the trees could feel all the tension release from inside her. The trees knew she had released the remnants of her old life and joined the forces of nature and the Cosmic. All was well!

Suddenly, a loud, piercing scream startled her. Someone needed some help. Papi jumped up, even though she was still woozy, and ran toward the screaming.

It sounded like it was down by the pond, so she headed off in that direction. It took a few minutes to get there. When she arrived, she saw two of the children from the third group standing on top of the beaver dam!

This was obviously not the smartest choice they had ever made. They were set on taking apart the dam so they could see where the beavers lived. However, the beavers were not happy with them trying to poke their noses in where they did not belong.

The beavers had come out of the home when they heard the kerfuffle outside, only to find the boys up to no good. They surrounded the children and began chiding them (in beaver language).

The beavers moved closer, trying to scare the children into stopping what they were doing and, hopefully, causing them to jump into the water so they could escape. The children were so fearful of the beavers; they froze in their tracks. When the beavers began chiding them, they broke into tears.

Papi walked right up to the dam, looking for a way to climb onto the snaggy surface. She wondered how these children had even gotten onto the dam without falling in the water.

She pushed right past the beavers and climbed onto the dam, then turned to face the beavers. When she turned, she realized Mama beaver was sitting on the shore, at the edge of the pond. She was watching the action going on, but she did nothing to take part in the fray.

Papi smiled at the beavers. They were her friends. She knew the children had committed a serious grievance. It needed to end right now! They needed to understand that the dam was the beavers' home, and they had no right to take it apart or stick their nose in where it did not belong.

Papi looked at the children and scolded them for the choice they had made, then took them by the hand and helped them climb off the dam. The beavers smiled back at Papi and made way for her and the children to return to shore.

Once Papi had them safely on shore, she returned to the top of the dam and proceeded to pull the discarded branches back on top of the dam. The beavers joined in, so in no time, one would never know there had been a situation.

Mama beaver smiled a huge beaver smile at Papi, and then, quick as a wink, Mama beaver became Rachel!

"*You have done it, my sweet Papillon!*" she said to her. "*You have acted in a completely selfless manner.*"

Before she even realized what Rachel had said, Papi became a golden butterfly again!

Papi flew up and down and all over the place. She looked like an acrobatic pilot at an airshow. Straight up into the heavens, then straight down, swooshing over the little beavers, then some rollovers above the children. Her golden butterfly was back!

The beavers were so excited by Papi's antics, they forgot they cannot stand on their hind legs. But they did! Just so they could clap and get crazy, celebrating the Golden Butterfly's return!

Rachel thanked the children and the beavers for doing their part in staging the event for her beloved Papillon. Now they could get down to business!

***

The meeting in the mind sanctum was still continuing on. They had not heard all the commotion outside because they were so absorbed in the conversation about how they needed to set something up to test Papi. Weren't they surprised when a little golden butterfly came shooting into their meeting!

Chapter 36

The third group of children is not to be forgotten. The Wind Surfers had truly become their mentors. It is amazing how much easier it is for children to learn when the teaching is being done by their peers rather than by adults.

The newcomers lapped up everything the gang taught them. It really excited them when Goose and Papi pulled off crazy stunts. They had become quite the entertainers! Their students loved them for it. No one ever knew what funny thing would happen that day.

Maintaining an environment of positive influences was the cornerstone of life in the Matrix. It was amazing to see the dramatic changes in a child when they received help to free themselves from their dysfunctional childhood beliefs.

The wounds they had carried from their old lives had flowed away into the ethers, being replaced by beliefs that helped them know they were amazing, unlimited creatures.

It excited the children to know that Papi had regained her wings. With no one else knowing, they had all being visualizing Papi flying around acting like an acrobatic pilot. They had their chests stuck right out when they heard the story of how Papi had rescued two of their pals from the beavers, and then put on a huge air show, just like they had visualized.

Each generation of children that had become part of the Matrix household was more integrated, and more adept in their abilities to live beyond the old perceived norm. They thrived on every lesson their teachers had bestowed on the earlier groups. They absorbed it all, just like they were a big old sea sponge!

It will be exciting when this group reached maturity!

They checked in as needed to assess whether any of the boys felt any kicking inside their bodies. Not one of them had felt the sensation. The boys and the girls just seemed to be ordinary kids with a huge zest for learning.

There was not one of them that could not do anything the Wind Surfers could do... well, except conjure up musical instruments! (Yet!)

For example, when they learned that the Wind Surfers could hold group meetings in the ethers by reaching out to each other, the Wind Surfers then had to figure how to block them from joining the meetings. Every time they knew a meeting was going on, they would show up too! The meetings stopped being like meetings, becoming more like conventions!

***

Merle was sitting out in the forest under a big old cedar tree. She closed her eyes to focus on one problem... How was she going to access other groups of children once they had arrested the man?

Keeping a continual flow of new children feeding this center, and one day at other locations was a key component of the work for the four originals. (Now that Mike, Merle, Tomas, and Tarita could work consciously with each other, we now have to consider them as four, even though they are really just two... you know what I mean!)

She was unparalleled in her skills in many of the mystical arts, such as telepathy, conjuring, mind reading. The one she had not figured out was how to get one step ahead of the man... and anyone else who was in his trade.

One skill she had learned, but forgotten, was how to project herself, body, and all, to wherever she wanted, and to be fully functional during the projection. It would also be helpful to project herself dressed for the part. Now, of course, anything that Merle could do, Mike was her partner, so he could play a part in it as well, but she was the stronger at doing these metaphysical practices, so he, just like on his motorcycle, was now on the back seat!

Clearing her mind as she sat by the tree, she opened her mind to the Universe, waiting for an answer. She sat there for a very long time, being receptive. She had learned to not allow limited thinking to creep in, as that was a guarantee of failure.

As she sat there, she felt someone sit down beside her. This person joined her in the peace of being connected with the Universe. Finally, she

decided it was time to get back to the building (Must
be near supper, her tummy was rumbling!)

When she opened her eyes, Condor was
sitting right next to her. She looked at him. "What
brings you here, Condor? I was not expecting anyone
to come to the garden. It surprises me to see you."

Condor smiled at Merle, then laughed. "You
adults have a lot to learn, let me tell you! We were all
sitting in the break room when we heard you asking
the Universe for help in figuring out how to project
wherever you like. We drew straws, and I got to
project to you. You know you grownups have such a
tendency to make things so difficult!"

"Whatever do you mean, Condor?" Merle
asked him. "Did you say that you projected yourself
here and that you all heard me petition the Cosmic?"

"It is not much different from the other times
you projected. Remember when you went to the town
where you got to work on that boat to get you to the
island? All you have to do to project is visualize
yourself there, and bingo, there you are!" he laughed.
"Why is that so hard to do? The only difference now is
what to wear, and that is easy to fix!"

With that, Condor took Merle by the hand, and an instant later they were sitting in chairs at a table with the rest of the gang in the break room. She looked down and realized she and Condor were wearing Viking outfits!

Merle looked at Condor and the others, shaking her head, then said, "Let's do that again!"

In the next second, they were sitting on the ground relaxing in a nearby park, wearing vintage clothing suitable for a day of picnicking in the park, watching the ducks swimming in the pond. By "they" in this case, meant all of them! It looked like they were having a school outing with the eight of them sitting there enjoying the sights, all wearing similar vintage outfits.

Merle looked around her, then she looked at Condor and laughed. "Now all we need is a picnic lunch!"

Condor raised his hand, swooshing it to the side. Then they all enjoyed some yummy sandwiches and big slices of cake and root beer.

***

Beth was doing her early rounds the next day, having a look at the home she had learned to love. It had been years now since each of the team had their own residences, so her early morning strolls had become walking about the Matrix instead of walking around the block at her old home.

As Beth approached the front door, she saw through the window glass that a young boy was sitting on something outside the door. He was looking toward the street, waiting for someone to notice him.

Beth opened the door, looking surprised, she said "Hello my young friend, what are you doing sitting there outside our door?"

He looked at her smiling and replied, "I am the boy that caught the golden butterfly at the orphanage a while ago. I was told to come here, so here I am."

"Oh!" Beth replied. "Who told you to come here? You must be starving. Come in, it is just about breakfast time."

As they walked to the breakfast room, he continued, "I kept having the same dream every night since the butterfly visited me. An angel in a violet gown kept calling me. She told me to go to the Matrix.

It is where you belong. I could not stop myself, so I set off to find this place. This angel said to tell you my name is Songbird. I guess it is because I like to sing like a bird!"

As he finished his story, they turned and walked into the cafeteria, where the morning meal was well underway. The gang was sitting together at a table near the door.

They heard the sounds of people coming into the room, so they looked over and all at once began yelling and hooting, "Songbird, Songbird, Songbird!"

And now the Wind Surfers were 8!

***

After Beth had checked with the orphanage, with the paperwork completed, Songbird became a full-fledged member of the Matrix and the Wind Surfers. The staff at his former home were glad he had found a new home, as he was always whistling like a bird!

Songbird settled in. The other members taught him how to do everything they could do. He was an adept student, so it did not take long until one would never know that he had not joined the Matrix crew at the same time as the rest of the gang. They even made sure he got his Wind Surfer T-shirt!

He told Beth during a conversation one day that when he caught Papi in the net; he felt something happen. Before that day, he was always looking for attention and would do anything to get it. He had even stolen that butterfly net from a local hobby store just so he would have something to wave around and get in other children's faces.

As soon as he had caught the little golden butterfly, he fell silent. He put the net away and stayed in his room, just sitting on his bed. For the first time in his life, he felt good, full, and connected. He kept looking at the jar that had contained the little butterfly, feeling sorry for capturing it. That is when the dreams started happening.

He said he could feel there were others like him, and they were nearby. When the angel came to him in his dreams and kept insisting that he needed to do as he was instructed, he packed his suitcase.

Songbird may not have fit well at the orphanage, but he fit in so well at the Matrix that no one would ever believe that he had not always been there!

***

Merle laughed at herself for wondering why she had thought it was such a big chore to solve her problem.

She chose to try projecting somewhere on her own. After successfully completing several trial runs with Condor, each time going further and further, she wanted to try one by herself.

"The distance is not a consideration for projecting," Condor told her. "After all, the projection is just a thought action, and the location is only a thought away. It would be important though to make sure that first, you are clear where you intend to land, and second, to make sure you have dressed appropriately. You don't want to be obvious by wearing the wrong outfit!"

Merle thought about it for a while, then decided she was ready, so she decided on a holiday at a cattle ranch. Riding motorcycles was fun, but she had always wanted to ride a horse and chase cows around!

When she arrived at the ranch, she looked down and saw herself in her new getup. The foreman looked at her and said, "You must be that new temp we ordered since Bill hurt himself. Hope you can ride well. We have a lot of work to do!"

And with that, he pointed at a horse for her and yelled, "Let's ride!"

Six cowboys were heading off to herd the cattle. She got on her horse and joined them. It was a good thing she was a fast learner because she had never seen a horse for real before this day, but she just watched the others and copied them. (She also had a quick chat with the horse, confessing she had never ridden before. It smiled and helped her out).

Cattle herding was a hard job, but she and the horse were one. In truth, she just rode the horse. The horse told her to let him just do his job, as he was an old pro at this game. No one ever knew the truth.

In a few days, Bill was ready to resume his job, so Merle thanked her new friends, then prepared to return home. A while after she had left, it dawned on the foreman that he had not seen how she had arrived... or left.

When she reappeared back at the Matrix, everyone cheered for her. Phoenix laughed at Merle, saying that he had especially enjoyed being inside a horse for a few days... although he had eaten quite enough hay and raw oats! He then went to his room, had a long shower. Heading to the cafeteria, he ate a meal that just about emptied the commissary! For once, Merle stood there, blank-faced!

Merle had become a force to reckon with. Now that she could project at will to anywhere she wanted and fit right in. It was time to make a plan. It was also time to ensure that Mike could also do projections and shift himself as well. After all, there may be a situation where he is present and needed to get out of there instantly... or sooner!

She did not feel ready yet to tackle dealing with the man. She also felt that she would benefit by organizing a group projection with the Wind Surfers so she could get the feel of working with multiple people at one time. Including Mike would be essential as well. What could she come up with?

She perused a national newspaper, looking for some inspiration. There must be something interesting they could do!

Then she found it! A city not far away was being wracked with riots. The people had taken insult that the local government had passed some very biased laws. The government had seen the errors in their thinking, but the people were still furious.

They filled the streets with angry mobs, so large that the police were becoming overwhelmed.

This was something she thought they could do something about, both with the mobs and with the people who attempted to push these unfair laws. Merle called the gang together and proposed a visit to this city by projection.

She suggested they needed to go right away before things got any worse. Hearing this, they all sat down and prepared, wielding authority to Merle so she could fly them to the city.

***

Everyone arrived safely, landing at the same place. Even Songbird had joined them! This was his first projection, so he was overjoyed, skittering around when he arrived. He was chirping and making quite the racket at first, but soon settled down so they could get to work.

Merle suggested they find a quiet place and get themselves prepared for the main event while she transitioned into Mike and went off to visit the police.

Mike introduced himself to the desk sergeant, who took him to the sergeant who was in charge of the riot squad.

"Yes, I have heard a lot about you, Mike. You created quite a reputation for yourself during the time you served. What are you wishing to speak with me about today? This is not a great time for social visits!" he laughed.

Mike laughed as well for a moment, then he explained why he was here in their town. "What I want to chat with you about is very serious. It will help you quieten things down around here."

The sergeant's ears perked up. "Go on. I really want to hear this."

So, Mike explained what his group was about to do and why in as few words as possible, as he was feeling a powerful pull to get back. With the sergeant's blessing, he was off and reunited with his gang.

As he arrived and rejoined as Merle, he saw why the feeling was so strong for him to get back. A large group of protesters were heading in their direction and did not seem to care about the havoc they were creating.

Merle got everyone to pull out their musical instruments. They all knew just what song to play, so it looked almost like someone had plugged in a CD.

The crowd kept coming toward them, looking very angry... well, for about another fifty feet!

As they reached a specific place, they stopped. It was just like someone had let the air out of some fancy balloons. Not one by one, but in unison, they all sat down, becoming quiet. They did not even speak to each other; they became mesmerized by the gentle music.

Smiles appeared on the faces of the rioters as they opened up to the music... and to Source. It was not long before they were humming along.

The riot police that had been trying to manage this group moved up to the front of the crowd when they arrived... created a new front row for the audience. The rioters smiled at them as they joined in on the humming.

This group was only a small part of the population that was infuriated, so Merle had them form a parade. With the riot police officers leading, all the former rioters followed suit, humming as they walked together.

Merle led the whole contingency right into the streets where the major rioting was going on. She had heard a story about a guy who had led a bunch of rats (or was it snakes?) out of Ireland a long time ago. She knew how he felt that day!

It was not long before the parade held thousands of people. Mike was searching through his memories of this city, trying to recall where there was a big enough park to hold all these people so they could get them off the street. He couldn't recall one, so he turned to Papi and sent her a thought to go find a park nearby.

Within a couple of minutes, she returned with the answer. Not far away was an enormous park with lots of green space.

Merle got the information as Mike did, so, under Papi's guidance, she steered the crowd in that direction. The gang ramped up the music to bolster the happiness of the crowd.

As they arrived in the park, the riot police that remained unaffected raced were there as well, expecting to deal with an immense problem. However, as the cheerful people trundled in behind their leader, they too joined in.

As she walked along, Merle broke into a fit of laughter! Surrounding the park were several catering trucks waiting to receive the crowd. She knew who the smart-aleck was that pulled that off!

When they arrived at the spot, they felt was the best place to continue the concert; she stepped aside to watch her gang. As they passed by, she saw Goose with a great big smile on his face, proud of his skill for telepathy!

Merle was not finished yet, though. There was still the other half of the problem. That was going to be Mike's job. She stepped out of sight for a minute, letting herself transform back into Mike. He headed off to speak to the people who had caused this entire problem.

He did not get very far though, because as he stepped out of the park, he noticed several limousines pull up. The perpetrators had heard what was going on and wanted to have a look at the situation.

If they had, or had not, intended to revoke the laws they had passed that caused this whole situation, no one will ever know. By the time they got themselves into the thick of the party, it had erupted into a giant, joyful event. They, too, were hypnotized by the music.

***

A few days later, after they had celebrated their victory in quelling the riot, the gang was all ready to go again. Merle had a fresh idea for them to test their skills.

It was going to be the Matrix version of a game called Capture the Flag.

They needed more people for this one, so they recruited some of the older members of the third group.

It was a good thing that Merle had included them because they were feeling pouty and left out after they had heard about what they pulled off in that riot-torn city!

The gang, now sixteen people, divided into two teams, with each member being given a flag. They tucked it into the back of their pants, so it hung down over their backside. The object of the game was for the players to grab the flag away from members of the other group. Once one team had collected all the flags from the other team, the game was over.

Merle was a little concerned that the team skill levels might be a little weighted toward the Wind Surfers. However, the Third Tier, as they became known, were not the least bit worried. They felt tenacity balanced out experience.

Each member had to keep his consciousness open so the other members of both his team and the other could track where they were. Otherwise, they could use whatever devices they desired to protect their flag. Once someone had removed their flag from their pants, they were to report back to the break room.

Merle's job in all this was to remain connected to each of the players, so she knew where they were and whether they still had their flag.

This exercise was to tell how well each of the members had integrated the skills they learned, and, of course, how well they complied with the rules of the game.

It was a good thing that there was a time limit placed on the game because it could have gone on forever! Once the members were dispatched, they all just disappeared into thin air.

The Wind Surfers had agreed to meet together in a building not far away so they could decide how to catch the other team before the game had even started. However, the Third Tier knew where they had gone, and sat outside waiting for them.

Not to be outdone, the Wind Surfers felt them outside and formed a huge force field around the building that pulled the Third Tier members tight up against the building like a wide belt. This gave them a chance to escape and head off somewhere else.

It was a good thing that Merle had added a couple of extra rules at the last moment.

They had to reappear on earth for at least one minute every ten minutes and they could not travel more than one hundred miles from the Matrix. Who knows where this game would have gone without these two rules! Mars anyone?

Once they had gotten themselves free of the energy belt, the Third Tier members blasted off to find the Wind Surfers. They were feeling like they were the followers, so they needed to come up with a strategy that would give them the advantage. But what?

In the meantime, they saw the Wind Surfers sitting in a cute little fluffy cloud up above them. They laughed, forming a powerful mind thought that turned the friendly little cloud into a very black, angry cloud. Then, just for effect, they threw in an eighty mile an hour wind that blew the cloud like a jet plane way out over the nearby mountains.

The Wind Surfers were not at all prepared for this event, so as the cloud containing them raised up to go over the mountains, they all fell out, leaving them exposed to the view of the Third Tier members.

Not to be outdone by these rookies, the Wind Surfers bound like a group of skydivers, and formed another energy wall around them, as well as a big air cushion on the ground below them, just for effect. When they landed, they each bounced gently to their feet.

The antics went on and on for the full two hours, with both teams becoming more and more creative. At the end of the two hours, not one person had stolen a flag.

Merle called them all back into the break room. No one had been ousted from the game!

They had worn themselves out from all the exertion, but they were proud of the skill they had shown.

"I am so proud of each one of you," Merle said to the crowd. "You have each shown exceptional skills, an impressive ability to work in unison, and you played fair. I could not have asked for more. You are all ready to take on more responsibility."

Shaking her head in wonder, she turned to the Third Tier members and said, "I just cannot believe how fast you people have learned your skills. I thought it was going to be a hands-down win for the Wind Surfers, but you held your own. You showed good strategic planning, good teamwork and you never once considered yourself disadvantaged."

At that point, the Wind Surfers jumped up and cheered and clapped for the Third Tier. Third Tier members, not to be outdone by their comrades, also jumped up and applauding the Wind Surfers. On and on it went, one group cheering for the other!

It seemed like nothing was going to stop the celebrating, so Merle signaled to Beth to bring in the celebratory drinks and food. She was going to say they needed music too, but, as always, when a thought went through her mind, the Wind Surfers knew.

It was a good thing there were no neighbors near the Matrix that day, as the celebration went on for hours, with everyone in the building now attending and celebrating.

Many, many hours later, with eyelids so heavy they could hardly see, everyone went off to bed.

***

The last test for everyone was a little trickier to set up as they could all read each other's minds, therefore making it difficult to do something that everyone would not know the answer to right away.

Merle decided the last challenge would be an individual test since a group is only as strong as any individual member. The first rule in this game was that no one could use their mind-reading skills on another member or staff.

Merle brought Teesha in to assist her. This would ensure that no one had an easy time because Teesha had not been trained to do projecting or receiving thoughts. Merle then taught her how to block her mind so no one could access her inner sanctum.

Teesha's job was to travel to three different locations, then place a piece of a puzzle in each. Teesha had complete freedom to choose where these puzzle pieces were to be placed. These pieces were very large and distinct, so once someone saw them, it would be easy to know they were the right pieces.

Merle told her to take her time in doing the tasks, and to take her time coming back just to make the task more challenging. Teesha was off!

A few days later, Teesha reappeared back at the Matrix. She looked refreshed and invigorated. Her job was complete, and now the challenge was ready for the members to play.

Merle gathered everyone together and gave them the instructions. It was game time!

Never following the rules, Papi called everyone together to discuss the upcoming game.

"I know they asked us to each work alone to win this competition, and I know I am risking my wings again, but I just want to say that I think we should work together to find these pieces. I think there are just too many variables to let each of us work on our own."

All the boys agreed with her, so they huddled in and decided what the strategy would be that would bring the right conclusion. By the end of the meeting, each person had a particular task to complete. Once they had figured out anything of value, they were to report to Papi.

Phoenix, for example, was to find out about Teesha's family, so they could research those locations to determine if she might have placed a piece with a family member.

Raven's job was to find out what places in nature that Teesha liked to enjoy.

Songbird decided he wanted to see if he could find out how she had traveled. As he walked toward the main entrance, he realized he had seen her leave the building when she set out on her journey. She had only her purse with her. She had no suitcase or other travel essentials.

He reported this to Papi and the rest of the members.

Papi opened the questions with this realization, "Songbird, what do you think that indicates?"

Songbird replied, "She did not leave town. She lives here at the Matrix, so if she were going somewhere far away, she would have taken a suitcase!"

Goose piped up, questioning, "Does this mean that the puzzle pieces are likely right here at the Matrix? Let's go look around outside!"

They all ran outside and fanned outside so they could search the whole backyard. It took only about thirty minutes until all three pieces were sitting on the table in the break room already assembled. The assembled pieces looked just like a full moon!

"Let's hang them up somewhere not obvious, but where someone who was looking for them could see them. We won't tell anyone, especially Merle or Teesha, that we have them already, and... let's go on a holiday of our own, pretending we are still looking for them!" suggested Phoenix. "I wonder how long it will take before Teesha comes out of her hiding place."

Everyone looked at Phoenix in shock, then smiled a mischievous smile when they thought about pulling off this prank.

"We have the free time anyway, so I agree with Phoenix. Let's do it!" whispered Hummingbird. "Where should we go?"

Falcon, not one of many words, suggested, "I heard about a concert on a beach that is starting soon. It would be neat to hear someone else's music, just for fun."

Everyone voted in affirmative, so it was set. Concert and beach! What a great idea, they all thought.

"Let's get this puzzle hidden in plain sight and be on our way then!" said Papi. "What could be a better combination than the ocean and glorious music! I hope my wings agree with salt water."

***

The next morning, Merle started her day with a casual walk through the halls of the Matrix. It was very unusual for it to be so quiet. She felt this would be a great time for a little rest of her own. This had been a very exciting, but exhausting, time for her and all the others. She strolled along looking at nothing in particular, looking in rooms, reminiscing about all the day-to day activities that go on when she noticed something new. It was a large picture hanging that was not there before, so she sauntered up to it to have a look.

"Why those sneaky little rats," she thought to herself. "They already figured it out and hid the puzzle pieces right in plain view."

Inside the picture frame was a picture of a bird with a chain hanging in its mouth with the three large jigsaw puzzle pieces dangling! There were other birds in the picture as well. They were singing to the bird with the chain. And what is that in the background? A beach?

"They found the puzzles where Teesha had left them in the back yard, then decided that since they have some spare time, they would go on a little vacation of their own," she said to Beth. "I think I will join them!"

***

It was pretty easy for more than thirty people of similar minds to have a lot of fun. It was especially easy to have fun in this group.

They had decided that they would build a camp down the beach from the concert site. It was close enough that they could hear the music without having to be at the concert. The music was so great. None of them had ever heard anyone else play music before, so it was a special treat for their ears.

"This will help us expand our repertoire," Goose said to everyone. "This is sure different from what we play!"

"It sure is!" laughed Merle as she walked into the campsite. "You guys! Going on vacation without me?" At that, she conjured up a beach chair and flopped into it.

They all stood there with a sheepish look on their faces while Merle settled herself in.

"What do you have to eat? Or do I have to make something myself?" she laughed as she held out her hand to them.

"Never mind," she said as she conjured up a portobello mushroom and Havarti cheeseburger with yam fries and a giant root beer. "We should do this more often!"

After they got over the shock of her arrival, they all laughed and continued with what they were doing. For many of them, this was the first time they had seen the ocean, so they were busy searching for seashells and other buried treasures or running into the waves as they crashed onto the beach.

After the concert wrapped up for the day, they were still ready to party some more, so they got out their musical instruments. They played what they had heard earlier in the day, so it wasn't long before a crowd gathered from the other campsites.

"You are doing a pretty good imitation of me there, Sunshine." came a voice from the newcomers.

Then another voice added, "Yah, you guys sound almost exactly like us. We didn't know we had a cover band! May we join you?"

Once they had their instruments, they went to plug in but could not find any electricity.

"How are you guys playing electrical instruments with no electricity?"

"We bring our own electricity. Just go ahead and play. Don't worry about the electricity. It will look after itself," laughed Goose.

The guy started playing his instrument without plugging in, and sure enough, it sounded just the way one would expect. At first, he had a very quizzical look on his face, but then he realized it did not matter, so he settled in and just played.

Nobody seemed to care that he didn't have his guitar plugged in, and soon the musician was so buried in his music that he forgot about it. By the end of the night, he had forgotten about this minor anomaly.

It was near daybreak by the time the crowd had died down. The musicians had played themselves out. The musician and his friends packed up and headed for their camps, ready for a good long sleep.

***

Just before the concert was to begin again later that day, the band leader returned to the campsite. He wanted the Wind Surfers to play with him at the concert. When he arrived, he could not believe his eyes. There was no evidence of there ever having been anyone in that area, never mind at least one hundred music-crazed campers!. There was not even a bit of litter on the ground! They had found the whole beach deserted, just like it had been a few days before.

Chapter 37

"It is time to get another load of kids to sell," thought the man. "This time I am going to get the job done myself. You know that old saying that if you want a job done right, you have to do it yourself!"

This was a move that he felt really uncomfortable with. In all the years he had been kidnapping children, he had always made sure that someone else was visible. That way, if things went sideways, no one would be the wiser about him. The front guys could always take the fall. After all, what was the point in him going to jail?

He let it out through his network that he was in the market for some more children. The buyers were always there, even though they were a little nervous after the last three failures. He assured them that things would be okay this time, as he was going to supervise the entire project personally from start to completion.

It only took a few days for the information he was looking for to come back to him. There was a great deal of fighting going on in a country not far away. The media had not been talking about it because this country was of little consequence to the economics of the world, so they had left them to fight each other in their quiet little corner with no bother.

"This is perfect," he thought to himself, "I need to stay off the radar, and since the media is not interested, it is likely they won't miss a few children then. I should be able to round up enough children to keep my buyers happy and get their concerns about me settled!"

So now that he had his target, he needed to round up a crew of associates who could help him with the job.

"Now, if I could just figure out who it was that was responsible for my last failures. I just could not find any information out about these people. I still don't even know if it was the same group that pulled off all three. Sure is mysterious how all those guys have just disappeared without a trace. I just do not get it."

"I am going to set up this new holding site so that no one can get in, or if they do, they won't be getting out. Then I can deal with them myself and get rid of them once and for all!" he muttered.

***

Mike was still watching for any information about this man. Interpol had been no help so far. He knew that before long, this man would start trying to make another play. Mike was going to keep his ears open and see if he could get the jump on him.

***

They say that those who have patience and determination will eventually succeed at their mission. One day, Mike received an encrypted message from a member of the Interpol team he had worked with while trying to discover what had happened to the boat captain. Once he could interpret it, he found what he was looking for. Even better, he learned that the man was planning to do the job himself and he was assembling a team to help him. It was now time for Mike to go on a trip!

Merle was excited too! She loved to travel, and she wanted to help catch this man. She had known he was moving forward with the next attempt for some time, but he had managed to elude her mind invasions enough that she did not get the information. That did not bother her at all. It was time to travel!

Mike and Merle had some discussions about how to proceed with catching this man before they set off.

"I think it might be a good idea for Tomas and Tarita to work with us on this project. More eyes and ears on the ground will be helpful. Besides, we might need Tarita's butterfly to do some reconnaissance!"

"That is a great idea, Merle, let's chat with them and get this organized. "We do not know who we will encounter this time, unlike the past events. I am sure he will be very careful about who he invites in with him."

"It's great that we will all be able to travel light this time since we have mastered this technique of projecting our bodies wherever we choose to go. However, we will need to make some transportation plans for the return trip since we will be bringing children with us. They likely won't be ready to teleport yet," laughed Merle.

It was going to take a lot of planning to pull this project together, but it was sure to be a success with the four of them working as a team again. Mike kept monitoring his system so he could keep up with any information that came out about the man and his plans.

Tomas, in the meantime, began researching about the country they would go to. They would need to be up to date with the war actions, the political situation, and the local transportation. They needed to understand everything beforehand to have a solid plan for moving the children out of the country once they had defeated the man and his gang.

The last thing to do was let Interpol know their plans and to message the federal immigration people that they should expect another group of children in the next few months.

**

Things had been going so well at the Matrix that they had almost forgotten about Rachel, although everyone knew she kept tabs on the ongoing evolution of the center and its inhabitants.

Mike called the staff together one morning so they could have counsel with her. Once everyone had settled in, Rachel appeared. As usual, it was like she had been waiting in the wings!

"*Good morning, my children. It is good to be with you this morning. I am so proud of the good works you have all been doing. The center is everything I knew it could be.*

It has been a wise choice to allow Rose to go on to other activities. This has certainly allowed each of you the room to mature into your most full purpose in the development and ongoing evolution of the Matrix. I see the growth in each of you as individuals. It gives me great pleasure.

Now, we are ready to embark upon a new adventure to retrieve another group of children that are ready to become Ascenders. We are truly thankful to this man for his good works. Although we all think of him as being evil for kidnapping the children, we would have a much more arduous task in front of us without him.

Unfortunately, this will be the last time we work with him as his life purpose will complete with this project, but fear not, there are many children and others that will benefit from your ongoing efforts.

It is very fortunate that the children here at the Matrix have been able to teach you so many new and useful tools. You will need all of them and more to complete the task ahead of you. Just remember that trust is your greatest tool!"

As Rachel concluded her message, she closed her eyes for a few moments and focused on her breath. She then opened her eyes with a new message.

"Before you travel to your new project, it is time for a graduation ceremony for all the Matrix children. Although they will continue to reside at the Matrix and grow through the many exercises we provide for them, it is necessary to give them recognition for their efforts.

Although, as adults, it is not as necessary to have the ego rewarded through recognition; it is still best for us to appreciate and recognize our children. It helps them to develop good self-esteem. We know good self-esteem aids the ego to relax, letting it be a beneficial tool rather than an obstacle to personal and spiritual development."

***

They gathered the children in the yoga room. They knew Rachel was coming this morning to speak with them. This was so exciting to the children they could hardly sit still in their seats.

They knew, though, when she appeared; they needed to sit and listen to the words she spoke. There were always important messages for them. This would be especially true today since the focus was on their own graduation.

As the children felt her presence nearing, they all became quiet and still. They closed their eyes and began focusing on their breaths. Soon, Rachel appeared in her beautiful lavender gown and wearing her most brilliant smile.

Rachel gazed upon the group for a few moments. She looked at each child, giving them singular recognition. Then she remained quiet for another few moments as she pulled the energy of the group into one.

"Good day to each one of you. I come here today to give recognition for your outstanding achievements. I can't believe that only a short time

ago, you were orphans lost in time. Now, you can look at yourselves as masters of your own destinies.

   The lessons you have received until now have been those dedicated for the minds of children. As of this day, you will receive training as adults regardless of your chronological age.

   Why? Because, in the eyes of the Cosmic, you have achieved so much in your few years breathing on this planet. It is felt you will grow even more quickly and completely if you view yourselves as adults. This does not mean the end of your childhood. Your child, or as we will now call it, your inner child, will live within you as part of your everyday life. You all have such wonderful abilities to enjoy and embrace this life that has evolved for you. Enjoy!

   It is through the eyes of a child that Heaven is attained. Therefore, retaining your child inside you is essential to your own well-being. When times seem difficult, your child can maintain presence in the now. Your inner child can both provide you with the information to resolve the situation and can also help you rebalance yourself.

The God we love is Universal. We call God by many names: Universe, God, Cosmic, Allah, and many more, but, in truth, God has no name. It is only our finite human mind that requires a word to label the concept of this unlimited power of which we are all a part.

The Universe grows through our own efforts to evolve. We are born into chaos. We feel the lack of love in our lives and the separation from one another. However, through our work in reframing our mind's understanding of our purpose in life, we come to know love through our connection with the Universe and as a product of our own coming to know our true selves.

There have been many great avatars in our time: Jesus the Christ and Buddha, to name two. There have also been many messengers and servants as the Cosmic has required from time to time, to accelerate the evolution of the oversoul of mankind.

Today, you begin your walk in your destiny, to shine among the stars just like Saint Francis of Assisi, Saint Germain, Mother Teresa, Gandhi, The Dalai

Lama, and thousands of other people throughout time.

Through the monumental works of these people, you will come to know even better the truth in the words of John 1:16 from the Christian Bible, when Jesus the Christ stated- I am the Way, the Light, and the Life.

The lesson you are learning is that Jesus, along with the other Great Leaders over time appeared on earth, not to suspend your evolution through fear, but to appear as living examples of what it means to be a True Servant of God living in the Glory of Love.

Your duty now is to be as Jesus The Christ has shown you by example. Be the Way, Be the Light, Be the Life. For as you shine the inner light of your soul outwardly to the world, you will lead others from darkness into the beautiful light that can only exist through complete immersion into the Cosmic Light.

As mature adults, you will now be able to face any demons that may still lurk deep inside you. Learn the lesson from this opportunity. Know all that exists is created in Love, therefore look at this lesson as an

*opportunity to increase your own vibration of Love.
Know the devil is your own ego. A powerful entity that
can work with you or against you, depending on how
you train it to respond to life.*

*It is your relationship with your own ego that
determines whether you live in heaven or hell, for they
do not exist outside your own mind. They are
perceptions created by your own understanding.*

*The greatest power you can bestow upon
yourself is by assisting another to become better, to
be more than they were before you knew them. There
is no true power in disempowering another through
acts of the ego. In fact, this act is disempowering to
you as well. When you interact with others, always
interact in the power of Universal Selfless Love.*

*The Cosmic has chosen you to aid the
consciousness of humankind. It is time for mankind to
let go of the indulgences of the ego and to embrace
and be absorbed into the Light. The energies of the
Universe are rapidly aligning to bring forward a new
level of consciousness. You are here to help those
who will choose to evolve, and to help those who
choose not. Ultimately, the choice is theirs what route*

they will take. Be not sad for those who choose to not come to the Light, for they will just sit aside until they awaken.

Some are ready to let go of the guardians they have placed in their minds, so they may join forces with you to become servants of the Universe. You will know them right away as you will see the beginnings of the light shining in their chests. If the light does not shine, then bless them and offer them tea.

Mankind has been blessed with the opportunity to grow and evolve, for it was through Divine Choice that Adam and Eve set the course of conscious evolution upon mankind. The choice they made was not a fall from Grace but an opportunity to support the Cosmic in its desire to grow and evolve. It is then by accepting and living in the Glory of God which we call Love that we Return to Grace."

As Rachel concluded her message, she closed her eyes and led the group in silent prayer. Then, as she re-opened her eyes; she smiled... Then she felt something touching her cheek...

"Oh, Papi!" she laughed.

~~The End~~ Beginning

A Message from Guardian Angel Rachel to our Beloved Readers

"I bring this story forward to share with you. It is a story of hope and illumination.

I am Rachel. I serve the Universal God that created this earth and all that exists. I invite you to join me in this moment of knowing yourself through the eyes of God.

With the ascending of the Age of Aquarius, Our Universal God desires that the human species become more aware of themselves, so they can evolve more quickly.

The Cosmic created our species as the medium for his own evolution, through self-awareness. With the culminating of the energies of transformation in each of the world's philosophics, These Cosmic energies indicate that now is the time for mass change.

This is a time of great stress on planet earth. Those who have not evolved spiritually find themselves motivated not by love, but by fear. These people focus on attaining power through control, manipulation, greed, or violence... all manifestations of fear.

The time is now, as the energies shift to embrace Universal Love as your primary life force. Only through this form of love can one become the true powerhouse they are created to be. This is not a simple task, as so much fear-based programming still runs at the forefront of the human mind.

The only path to embracing and living in true love is found through self-recognition and self-knowledge beyond the ego's concept of who you are. Know Thyself.

You, like every human that ever existed, have a specific purpose to fulfill in this life. That special purpose can only be found by moving past the lessons of childhood one has learned that distort the truth about life and about your own self-perception.

This time that is now present is not a time for fear. It is not a time for limitation. It is a time to find and embrace the real you, the one that lives and expresses limitless truth and love, the way that the God of your Heart manifested you to be.

No matter your personal relationship with what we call Universal Consciousness. No matter whether you believe your God to be male, female, or of no gender. No matter if you call your God by any name, or you do not believe that God even exists at all. Now is the time to let go and be open to the concept that there is a place for you that is much greater than your own limited understanding of yourself and your reason for living at this particular time.

I invite you to join me in the lessons of this story. Let yourself be a part of this journey as if you are one of the loved ones you read about.

Take to heart the lessons incorporated herein as an opportunity for you to advance your own personal journey into yourself.

As this story completes, you will find, if you allow yourself to embrace the messages in this offering, you will be happier, feel more complete, and enjoy a more peaceful expression of yourself. You will know that everything is good. You will have replaced the old fear-based beliefs with the Love that is and always was yours.

Let this story inspire you to journey into yourself, to transition yourself beyond the illusion of fear. Let yourself embrace change for your own good through the loving energy that caused you to be created at this time. You are born to be amazing and powerful. You just have to accept yourself, and the Universe is yours!

In the name of Divine Love, I make this offering to each one of you!"

Would you like a free book?

Thank you for buying my book, The Ascenders Return To Grace Book 1.

I hope you have enjoyed this story as much as I had fun writing it. As a thank you for your purchase, I have 2 gifts for you.

The first gift you will find right after this section. It is a sneak peek into Book 2.

With the second gift, you can reach into my non-fiction world of writing. This little book is chock full of concepts focused on raising healthy children.

It is called

Healthy Children Only Need Three Things.

Since The Ascenders Return To Grace Book 1 is focused on saving kids from a kidnapping group, then helping them to heal, I thought this would be a fitting gift.

It is this easy to receive this book. Simply go to my website www.montyritchings.com/freebook , click the access link and sign up for my email list that way. The book is yours. That easy! You will find it in your email box.

Being a member of my personal book club, you will now be able to stay in touch with me and my work. I will update you on new events, discount book offerings and new books as they develop.

Don't worry, you can always unsubscribe if you're no longer interested.

Writing a novel is fun, but it also can be a hard and daunting task, especially to make sure a lot of readers will find it and read it. Your support by joining my email list, goes a long way to encourage me to keep going. Who knows what surprises might evolve!

If you like this book, then please leave an honest review on your favorite review site afterward. I love to read what you think. Your honest review is essential to the process of keeping the books coming.

For now: enjoy this rollercoaster.

Monty C. Ritchings

Here is a Sneak peek of Book 2
Chapter 1

Mike pondered the biggest question he had needed to answer in recent memory…. as he sat on the seat of his vintage Harley-Davidson motorcycle. It brought back so many memories to just sit there, recalling all the cold cases he had solved back so many years ago, hoping for some inspiration.

Today was a different world though, as he sat in front of the abandoned bar where he and Tomas had ousted a motorcycle gang that had taken the bar hostage as their clubhouse… at least until Tomas used it to show off his skill at using his positive energy to reframe bad situations.

Today was different as well in one other very significant way…. Mike was not just Mike! He was one of the first of a new breed of human beings. They were called Homo integratis. He was sitting in front of this abandoned bar because… Merle suggested it.

Who was Merle? She is his fully integrated female half. He and Merle shared the same body, sort of. Sometimes Mike looked like Mike as a guy and sometimes he found himself re-invented into a female (including her body) named Merle. They had learned to get along with each other. It took a while, but since they kind of had to travel everywhere together, they had little choice, so during a break from being part of the team at the Matrix, they had learned how to talk with each other and conceded that since they share the same body, they better learn to work together and like it!

Now, sitting on his motorcycle, Mike pondered, Merle pondered. She thought it would be helpful if they rode over to this old bar to reconnect with the energy to figure out where the leader of that gang had disappeared to.

Why might you ask?

Merle thought they might get some ideas from this man about how to create a cover. The bad man from whom they had rescued not one, not two, but three large groups of children that he had captured and sold off into slavery was preparing to capture a fourth set. This time, he was going to do the job himself, since everyone else seemed so incapable of pulling off the jobs the way he wanted.

Three times they had relieved him of his property! All three times, his people had disappeared, never to be found again. The whole situation baffled the bad man, but he was determined that this mission was going to be done right this time, that his clients would forget about his past.

Merle felt that if they could find the leader of this gang, who supposedly knew this guy might be of service to Mike and Merle. Or maybe, once they find him, he should get another dose of Tomas' amazing energy! No, that was not the way things worked for members of Homo integratis. Everything they completed was done with the highest of intentions, so they just needed to ensure that he will cooperate on his own.

As they continued to ponder, Merle drew the scene of the bikers wreaking havoc in the bar. Then she drew a picture of Tomas washing the bikers with golden light, the power of Universal Love.

Then, as Mike sat looking around, who did he see wandering up the street but the gang leader!

"Merle, you lovely creature, you did it again!" Mike laughed as he felt a kick in his side (from the inside). Then he heard a loud snicker from inside too as Merle looked out, transforming herself to the outside. She looked ravishing in her black leathers. Who wouldn't want to stop to chat with her, especially a former leader of a notorious motorcycle gang?

As he walked up, Merle noted as he came into view, that he looked as much as a motorcycle gang leader as a chicken looked like a monkey! She knew it was him though, because she could read his energy imprint. Even though his life had been transformed that fateful day, she knew it was him.

"Hello, Lindsay!" Merle smiled at him as he walked by.

Lindsay looked upon her shocked as she addressed him, trying to figure out if he should know her.

Lindsay smiled (Who wouldn't be, looking at this beauty!), and then asked her, "How do you know my name, there beautiful?" He stood nearby on the sidewalk, not moving toward her, just waiting.

"I know a lot about you, Lindsay. Have you time to chat with me? You might have some information I need." She replied.

"This is too weird," Lindsay muttered, more to himself than to Merle. "I was walking down a street not far from here going to meet some friends for coffee when I got the urge to walk over this way. Then I come walking along here and you are sitting here waiting for me. Don't you find that a little weird? I am sorry, you know my name, but I do not know yours… or what information I might have that you may need. Nice bike, by the way!"

"Life does have these moments, doesn't it?" she laughed at him, then reached out her hand to him. "My name is Merle. I apologize if this seems so unsettling to you. I am sure though that you have had other strange occurrences near here at some time."

Lindsay looked around and shrugged his shoulders. "Can't say I have had much to do with this area, but there have been some strange occurrences in my life."

"Let me help you recall, my friend," and with that, she projected some special energy into his hand as they connected. He bounced backwards, like he had shaken hands with a bolt of lightning, landing on his back on the sidewalk.

"What did you do, Merle? I have felt nothing like that before," he replied as he picked himself up. "I do remember this area now! It's funny, until this moment, my mind would only go back a few years, then everything went fuzzy. I remember waking up one day knowing I had to go back to school, so I did. Now I am almost finished becoming a special education teacher."

Merle smiled at him, saying "You are now living your true destiny, Lindsay. You had a life before that was so far off base from what you were born to do. You might say friends of mine helped you find your way."

Lindsay smiled and said, "I am glad they did. I can now recall everything. It all came back, just like it was never gone. My childhood was really rough. I had to raise myself and I guess I did not do a very good job of it. I got into a lot of trouble when I was a kid, so it wasn't much of a stretch to become a member of a notorious motorcycle gang. I think they called me Dorf. It is a shortened version of my last name. I guess I could not be very notorious with a name like Lindsay, could I?"

"So what can I help you with, Merle?" he asked.

Merle explained without going into deep detail about the mission she was on. She was going to rescue some children being kidnapped by a man who had worked with a local group of thugs that hung out down by the waterfront. She was putting together the mission, but needed more information about this man so they could offer their services to him.

"I can tell you lots about him, and I would love to be involved. This guy has to be stopped," he replied.

Almost on cue, they could hear the roaring of motorcycles racing toward them. Both Merle and Lindsay jumped from the noise, then stood waiting, looking up the street.

Seven vintage Harleys, all identical to the one Merle rested on, pulled up beside her. The leader stopped, pulling his bike up right beside her. He then stared at her for a moment and then laughed.

"Oh Goose, you scared us." Merle laughed. "This is Lindsay. He used to be the leader in a notorious motorcycle gang."

"Bad as us?" Goose said with a grin from ear to ear, looking at Lindsay.

Lindsay just stood there and stared, not sure what to do or say. These guys looked really tough, and he did not want to go back to that time in his life again for anything.

Merle looked at Lindsay, almost apologetically, then said to him, "Lindsay, meet Goose. You have a lot to learn. This was quite unexpected, but if you are willing, and have the time right now, you are going to get the ride of your life!"

Lindsay looked at Goose again, then at Merle, as he jumped on the back of Merle's motorcycle.

"I don't know what I am in for, but there is something about you, Merle, that I know I can trust, so let's go. Guess my friends will have to have their visit without me!" Lindsay laughed as they rode off with a roar.

"Wind Surfers, eh? Doesn't sound very notorious!" Lindsay said to Merle, pointing at the colors on the jackets of the other riders.

Acknowledgements

It is with heartfelt thanks I acknowledge all the great people who inspired and assisted me in the creation and completion of this book. In particular, Cheryl Brewster whose intuitive coaching brought forward the aspect of me who needed to get this story on paper, Garth Twa and my sister Trish Clark for keeping me going and Judith Hunter for the proofreading insights.

I dedicate this book to truth and inspiration, aspects of the Universal mind that open the door to creativity. May we all grow to be the amazing people we truly are.

I also reach out to the fellow authors who have inspired me over my life to become a visionary and intuitive: Richard Bach, Carolyn Myss, Louise Hay, John Welwood, James Redfield, Shirley MacLaine, Gary Zukav and many, many more.

Thank you!

About the Author

Monty has long had a passion for the esoteric world. Being a member of The Rosicrucian Order AMORC since 1981, he has been able to develop a good knowledge base, both theoretical and practical of both the mundane and esoteric worlds.

He has also studied Core Belief Engineering, Mind Dynamics, Heart Resonance Therapy, Jin Shin Jyutsu, and Reiki plus he has developed a connection with source that has provided some other practical intuitive healing techniques.

Monty's interest in the non-physical side of healing began with a program he studied at Douglas College in New Westminster BC Canada back in 1970 called Human Development. It was offered by two very open minded social workers. It was the beginning of his never ending quest to understand the human mind and its impact on people's lives from an intuitive perspective.

Monty is also a seasoned public speaker having completed the Competent Toastmaster level three times plus the Able Toastmaster level in Toastmasters International, where he wrote and facilitated many workshops and keynote talks. In fact, his love for writing books came from writing speeches in Toastmasters.

Monty's passions are human evolution, nature and traveling. Monty has walked the complete Camino Frances Trail (500 miles) from St Jean Pied de Port to Santiago de Compostela in Spain in 2015 and 2017. He says he still has at least one more in him!

Monty lives in Langley BC Canada

Corporate name: Life Force Creative Inc.

Other Books by Monty C. Ritchings

- **Embracing The Blend -** (2007. 2010, 2023)
  What Mom and Dad Didn't Know They
  Were Teaching You
- **Stamp Out Stress** - (2009)
  Living With Stress is a Choice, Not a fact of Life
- **Chakras Demystified** – (2014)
  Our True Communication System Revealed
- **Healthy Children Only Need Three Things** (2018)
- **Let's Get Hiking** (2018)
  A Guide for Long Distance Hikers and Walkers

Website: **https://montyritchings.com**

Namaste